"Why?" Jake asked in a hoarse whisper. "Why didn't you come back to me?"

"Because I *don't* know you," she cried.

"You believe that stuff in the envelope about me? Even after that kiss?"

"No. Jake, I don't remember anything before waking up in a hospital six years ago."

"You don't still believe you're Isabella Montenegro?"

"How can I after everything that's happened? After—" The kiss. She unconsciously ran her tongue over her upper lip, the memory still fresh, the feeling still intoxicating.

"But you're afraid of me because of what you found in the envelope."

"I don't know who or what to believe at this point," she said, looking away.

"If you could remember what you and I had, you'd know the truth," Jake said softly. "I loved Abby Diaz. We were going to get married. We were going to have a child."

"We *did* have a child...."

Dear Harlequin Intrigue Reader,

It's autumn, and there's no better time to *fall* in love with Harlequin Intrigue!

Book two of TEXAS CONFIDENTIAL, *The Agent's Secret Child* (#585) by B.J. Daniels, will thrill you with heart-stopping suspense and passion. When secret agent Jake Cantrell is sent to retrieve a Colombian gangster's widow and her little girl, he is shocked to find the woman he'd once loved and lost—and a child who called him *Daddy*....

Nick Travis had hired missing persons expert Taryn Scott to find a client, in Debbi Rawlins's SECRET IDENTITY story, *Her Mysterious Stranger* (#587). Working so closely with the secretive Nick was dangerous to Taryn's life, for her heart was his for the taking. But when his secrets put her life at risk, Nick had no choice but to put himself in the line of fire to protect her.

Susan Kearney begins her new Western trilogy, THE SUTTON BABIES, with *Cradle Will Rock* (#586). When a family of Colorado ranchers is besieged by a secret enemy, will they be able to preserve the one thing that matters most—a future for their children?

New author Julie Miller knows all a woman needs is *One Good Man* (#588). Casey Maynard had suffered a vicious attack that scarred not only her body, but her soul. Shut up in a dreary mansion, she and sexy Mitch Taylor, the cop assigned to protect her, strike sparks off each other. Could Mitch save her when a stalker returned to finish the job? This book is truly a spine-tingling pager-turner!

As always, Harlequin Intrigue is committed to giving readers the best in romantic suspense. Next month, watch for releases from your favorite special promotions—TEXAS CONFIDENTIAL, THE SUTTON BABIES, MORE MEN OF MYSTERY and SECRET IDENTITY!

Sincerely,

Denise O'Sullivan
Associate Senior Editor
Harlequin Intrigue

THE AGENT'S SECRET CHILD
B.J. DANIELS

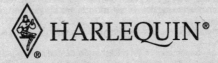

HARLEQUIN®

TORONTO • NEW YORK • LONDON
AMSTERDAM • PARIS • SYDNEY • HAMBURG
STOCKHOLM • ATHENS • TOKYO • MILAN • MADRID
PRAGUE • WARSAW • BUDAPEST • AUCKLAND

Special thanks and acknowledgment are given to
B.J. Daniels for her contribution
to the Texas Confidential miniseries.

ISBN 0-373-22585-7

THE AGENT'S SECRET CHILD

Copyright © 2000 by Harlequin Books S.A.

This edition published by arrangement with Harlequin Books S.A.

® and TM are trademarks of the publisher. Trademarks indicated with
® are registered in the United States Patent and Trademark Office, the
Canadian Trade Marks Office and in other countries.

Visit us at www.eHarlequin.com

Printed in U.S.A.

ABOUT THE AUTHOR

Born in Houston, B.J. Daniels is a former Southern girl who grew up on the smell of Gulf sea air and Southern cooking. But her home is now in Montana, not far from Big Sky, where she snowboards in the winters and boats in the summers with her husband and daughters. She does miss gumbo and Texas barbecue, though! Her first Harlequin Intrigue novel was nominated for the *Romantic Times Magazine* Reviewer's Choice Award for best first book and best Harlequin Intrigue. She is a member of Romance Writers of America, Heart of Montana and Bozeman Writers Group. B.J. loves to hear from readers. Write to her at: P.O. Box 183, Bozeman, MT 59771.

Books by B.J. Daniels

The Confidential Agent's Pledge

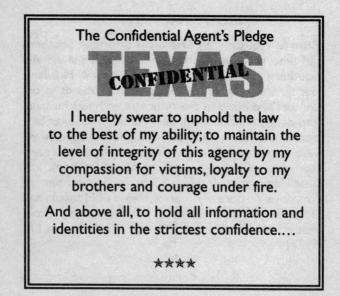

I hereby swear to uphold the law
to the best of my ability; to maintain the
level of integrity of this agency by my
compassion for victims, loyalty to my
brothers and courage under fire.

And above all, to hold all information and
identities in the strictest confidence....

★★★★

CAST OF CHARACTERS

Isabella Montenegro/Abby Diaz—Was she the former FBI agent who everyone believed was dead? Then why couldn't she remember who'd tried to kill her? Worse, why couldn't she remember the man she'd supposedly loved?

Jake Cantrell—His job as an agent for Texas Confidential was to find a woman and child. But he found a lot more.

Elena Montenegro—All the five-year-old had ever wanted was a father.

Julio Montenegro—He knew the truth, but he got greedy and it cost him his life.

Tomaso Calderone—The drug lord thought he'd found his chance to get Jake Cantrell.

Dell Harper—He'd been like a little brother to Abby. But how well had she known him?

Ramon Hernandez—As Calderone's right-hand man, he had to stop Abby and Jake—or die trying.

Frank Jordan—The past had come back to haunt him. And now it was just a matter of time before the truth got out.

Tommy Barnett—He'd do anything for a friend. Even kill.

Reese Ramsey—He was the only agent from the past who Jake could trust. But was that trust misplaced?

Crystal Winfrey Jordan—She had a very good reason to be jealous of Abby Diaz. But what was that reason?

This book is dedicated to my aunt,
Lenore Collmorgen Bateman (1912-1999).
I never think of Texas without thinking of her.
Some of my fondest memories are of her making
pancakes over a Coleman, joking and laughing.
She was a great cook and one of the strong women
in my life I have tried to emulate.

Prologue

She smelled smoke. Just moments before, she'd been helping her daughter Elena look for her lost doll. Now, she stopped, alarmed. Her hand went to the small scars at her temple, memory of the fire and the pain sending panic racing through her. Why would Julio build a fire on such a hot spring day in Mexico?

Then she heard the raised voices below her in the kitchen and the heavy, unfamiliar tread on the stairs.

The feeling came in a rush. Strong, sure, knowing, like only one she'd ever felt before. And yet she trusted this one. Whoever was coming up the stairs intended to harm her and her five-year-old daughter.

Fear paralyzed her as she realized she and Elena were trapped on the second floor. The only way out was the stairs the man now climbed. Her husband had barred the windows and he had the only key. She'd often wondered: what if there was another house fire and Julio wasn't home?

But Julio always left someone to watch over them when he was gone.

The lumbering footsteps reached the second-floor landing. She shot her daughter a silent warning as she scooped the child into her arms and hurried to the attic stairs at the back of the house.

Her heart lunged in her chest as she moved through the hot cluttered attic, frantically searching for a place to hide. She found the only space large enough for the two of them in a dark corner behind an old bureau where the roof pitched out over the eave and a pile of old lumber formed a small partition.

She could hear the men ransacking the house, their voices raised in angry Spanish she couldn't make out.

When she heard the plodding tread on the attic stairs, she'd motioned to Elena to keep silent but the child's wide-eyed look told her that she understood their danger, just as she always had.

The man was in the attic now, moving slowly, carefully. The other men called to him, their feet thumping on the steps as they hurried up to him.

"Where is Isabella and the child?" one of the men demanded in Spanish. He had a quick, nervous voice like the brightly colored hummingbirds flickering in the bougainvillea outside the window.

"I don't know," a deeper voice answered. "Montenegro must have gotten them out before we arrived."

"Damn Julio. Find the money. Tear the place apart if you have to, but find the money."

"What if he gave it to her?" one of them asked, only to be answered with a curse.

As the men searched the house, she hugged her daughter tightly, determined to protect her child as she had since Elena's birth, feeling as defenseless and trapped as she always had.

The men eventually searched the attic, including the bureau drawers, while she'd held her breath and prayed they wouldn't find her and Elena crouched in the darkness and dust.

She took hope when she sensed the men were losing momentum, their movements less frantic but no less angry and frustrated.

"He wouldn't hide it in the house," one of the men snapped in Spanish. "He was too smart for that. So why are we wasting our time? He gave it to the woman and kid to hide somewhere for him."

"Shut up!" the nervous one growled. "Keep searching." But he said it as he tromped back down the stairs and soon the others followed.

She waited until she thought they'd left before she crept from the hiding place and stole with her daughter down one floor to her bedroom. With a chilling calm that frightened her more than the men had, she packed a bag with a few belongings.

She started at a noise behind her. Click, click, click. Someone was still downstairs, she thought, glancing at the phone beside her bed. It was making that faint clicking sound as the extension downstairs was being dialed.

With that same cold calm, she carefully picked up the extension. Two voices. One coarse as sand. The other nervous and quick and now familiar.

"I want my money, Ramon," the coarse one snarled.

"The woman must have taken it and the child with her."

"Find them. Make them tell you where Julio hid the money he stole from me. Then bring them and the money to me. *Comprende?*"

"*Si*, Señor Calderone, I understand." The man named Ramon promised on his dead mother's grave.

She hung up the phone and finished packing. Since the day she'd awakened in the hospital after the house fire to find Julio beside her bed, she'd suspected her husband was involved with drug lord Tomaso Calderone.

She'd awakened in pain. From her injuries and the surgeries. From the confusion in her mind.

But it was awakening to find herself pregnant that made her close her eyes and ears to Julio's dealings, thinking only of her baby, her sweet precious daughter. Julio had never shown any interest in either of them, leaving her alone to cook and clean and raise the child he wanted nothing to do with.

Once she got some of her strength back physically and Elena was old enough to travel, she'd tried to leave her marriage. But Julio had caught her and brought her back, warning her that she and Elena could never leave. They were his and he would rather see them both dead than ever let them go.

She had looked into Julio Montenegro's eyes and known then that he felt nothing for her or Elena, something she had long suspected. She and Elena were his prisoners for reasons she could not understand. But for Elena's sake, she'd never tried to escape again.

Instead, without realizing it, she'd been biding her time, waiting. She hadn't known what she'd been waiting for. Until today.

With the bag in one hand and Elena's small hand in the other, she crept down the stairs as soon as the lower floor grew silent again.

Julio lay sprawled on the white tile floor of the kitchen in a pool of blood, his eyes blank, his body lifeless.

Shielding Elena from the sight, Isabella moved to him, her gaze not on his face, but on the knife sticking out of his chest.

With a cold, calculating detachment she hadn't known she possessed, she grasped the knife handle in both hands, and pulled it from her husband's chest. Then she calmly wiped the knife clean on his shirt and slipped the slim blade into her bag.

She looked down at his face for a moment, wishing she felt something. Then, like a sleepwalker, she knelt and searched his pockets, lifting him enough to remove the small wad of pesos his business associates had obviously passed up as too trivial to bother with from his hip pocket.

It wasn't much money. Not nearly enough to get her and Elena out of Mexico, let alone to some place safe in the States. But was there any place safe from Calderone and his men?

She started to rise, then noticed that when she'd lifted Julio, she'd also lifted the edge of the rug under him. The corner of a manila envelope was now visible beneath the rug.

With that same chilling calm, she raised Julio enough to free the parcel from beneath him and the rug. She stared at the large envelope, then the fire he'd built in the stove. Had he been planning to burn the envelope? Why else would he have built a fire in a room already unbearably hot?

She looked again at the envelope. She knew it didn't contain the missing money. It was too lightweight, too thin, to hold the amount of money she feared Julio had stolen. But maybe it had information about where he'd hidden the drug money. Why else would he try to burn it just before he'd been killed, if not to protect his ill-gotten gains?

She grasped the hope. If she had the location of the stolen money, then maybe she could buy her freedom and her daughter's from Calderone.

As she lifted the parcel to look inside, something fell out and tinkled to the tiles. The tiny object rolled to a stop and as she stopped to pick it up, she saw that it was a silver heart-shaped locket. It had no chain and the silver was tarnished and scratched, making it hard at first to read the name engraved on it.

Abby.

She stared at the locket. Should that name mean something to her? Was it one of her husband's mistresses? One of her lost relatives?

She pried the two halves open and stared down at a man's photo inside, her fingers trembling. Not Julio. Not any man she'd ever seen before. She felt Elena beside her and tried to shield her from the body on the floor, but saw that her daughter was more interested in the locket—and the photo inside.

"Papacito," Elena whispered, eyes wide as she stared down at the photo of the stranger.

"No, my little bright angel," she said softly, sick inside. For the first time, she let herself hate Julio. She'd never wanted him as a husband, but he could have been a father to Elena, who desperately needed a father's love.

Instead their daughter preferred to believe a total stranger in a small black-and-white photograph was her father rather than Julio Montenegro, the unfeeling man who'd given her life.

A car backfired outside, making her jump. Hurriedly, she shoved the locket back into the envelope with the official-looking papers. Like the weapon she'd taken from Julio's chest, she put the parcel into her bag. As she turned to leave, she saw her daughter's lost rag doll and, wondering absently how it had gotten there, she scooped it up from the floor, took her daughter's small hand, and ran.

JAKE CANTRELL stood back, sipping his beer, watching the wedding reception as if through binoculars.

The Smoking Barrel Ranch had taken on a sound and feel and level of gaiety that seemed surreal, as if it had an alternate personality—one he didn't recognize.

He hadn't been brought here for this and right now, he just wanted it to be over. Not that he wasn't happy for Brady and Grace...now Catherine. He was. He just didn't believe in happy-ever-after anymore. Mostly, he told himself, he was just anxious to get back to work.

But that was a lie. All day he'd felt an uneasiness he couldn't shake. Like when he felt someone following him or waiting for him in a dark alley. The feeling hummed like a low-pitched vibration inside him, making him anxious and irritable and wary.

Mitchell had called a meeting later tonight. Jake wanted a new assignment, something that would take him away from the ranch for a while. Away from everything. Work kept him sane—relatively sane. It was also the only thing that kept him from dwelling on the past.

He felt eyes on him. Not just watching him. But staring at him. He shifted his gaze and saw Penny Archer across the room, standing with her back to the library door she'd just closed behind her. Earlier he'd noticed when she'd gotten a beep on the priority line. Noticing was something he was good at. That and finding people who didn't want to be found.

It had to have been a business call. That was the

only kind that would make the administrative assistant leave the wedding reception and the boisterous crowd, and disappear into the library. From there the hidden elevator would take her to the basement and the secret office of Texas Confidential. The true heart of the ranch. Its aberrant split personality.

Now he met Penny's intent gaze and felt a jolt. She was as tough as they came. It took a lot to upset her. And right now, she was visibly upset.

He made his way across the room, knowing it had been the priority call that had upset her. Just as he knew the call had to do with him.

"What?" he asked, never one to mince words.

She motioned for him to follow and led him away from the crowd and the noise of the party, outside to a corner of the porch. In the distance, mesquite stood dark-limbed against the horizon, shadows piled cool and deep beneath them. The land beyond was as vast and open as the night sky.

"I just got the strangest call," she said the moment they were alone and out of earshot of the others. Her gaze came up to his. "It was from a little girl. A child. No more than three or four. She spoke Spanish and—" Penny's voice broke. "She was crying. She sounded really scared, Jake."

"What did she want?" he asked, wondering what this could possibly have to do with him.

"She said her mommy was in trouble and needed help. She asked for her daddy." Penny seemed to hesitate. "Her daddy Jake."

He felt a chill even as a warm Texas wind whispered through the May night. He shook his head. A mistake. A wrong number. An odd coincidence.

"Jake, she called through your old FBI contact number."

He stared, his heart now a sledgehammer. Only three people in the world had ever known that number and two of them were dead. "What did she say? Exactly." Not that he had to add that. Penny could remember conversations verbatim. That was part of her charm—and the reason the thirty-four-year-old was Mitchell Forbes's right-hand woman.

She repeated the Spanish words. "Then I heard a woman's voice in the background. The woman cried, *'No, chica suena.'* Then the line went dead. Of course, I put a trace on the call immediately. It came from a small motel on the other side of the Mexican border."

Chica suena. The light in the trees seemed to shift. Lighter to darker. The porch under him no longer felt solid, became a swampland of deadly potholes. His world, the fragile one he'd made for himself here, spun on the edge of out of control. Just as it had six years ago. Before Mitchell had saved him.

From far off, he heard Penny ask, "Jake, are you all right? Jake?"

Chica suena. He hadn't heard the unusual Spanish endearment in years. Six long years. Nor was it one he'd ever heard before he'd met Abby Diaz. It was something her grandmother had called her. It meant "my little dream girl." And it suited Abby.

Abby Diaz had been everything to him. The woman he was to marry. His FBI partner. His most trusted friend.

His *chica suena.*

He bounded off the porch, his long legs carrying him away from the party and the faint sound of music and laughter. Away from the pain and anger and memory of the death of his dreams of love ever after. Away. But he knew, gut-deep, that running wouldn't help. It never had.

Someone had found out about him and Abby. Had found out their most intimate secret. Daddy Jake. *Chica suena.* Someone wanted him running scared again. And they'd succeeded.

Chapter One

Isabella Montenegro lay on the bed, her body drenched in sweat, fear choking off her breath. Dark shadows shifted in the shabby motel room, one image refusing to fade—the image of her husband Julio sprawled in a pool of blood on the kitchen floor. But it was the knife sticking out of his chest, rather than his blank eyes, that she saw so clearly.

She shuddered, watching herself pull the knife from his chest. She watched it in her mind's eye, watched the unfeeling woman wipe the blade clean on his shirt, then slip the weapon into her bag.

She closed her eyes. Who was that unfeeling woman? Or had she always been this cold, this uncaring?

Yes, she thought, unable to recall the other feeling, the only other strong, sure, knowing one she'd ever had, one she hadn't trusted. A feeling that she'd known earth-shaking passion.

A lie, she thought. She'd never known passion. Not with Julio, who'd never been a husband to her.

Not with anyone. She couldn't even call up the feeling.

She closed her eyes to the horrible image of her moving his body to retrieve the envelope. But the image danced in the darkness behind her eyelids, taunting her. What kind of woman was she?

She opened her eyes and snapped on the lamp beside her bed, chasing the shadows from the cramped room and illuminating the tiny body sleeping next to her.

Elena was curled in a fetal position, her small, warm back against her mother's side, her dark hair hiding her face.

She had done it for Elena, she told herself now as she sat up, careful not to wake her daughter. Everything she'd done, she'd done for Elena.

Only now they were running for their lives. Scared, with no one to turn to and nowhere to go. Her sleepless hours filled her with nightmares. Not of the men chasing her and her daughter, but of the memory of the emotionless woman who'd pulled the knife from her husband's chest, then calmly picked up her daughter's doll and left without looking back.

What had she planned to do with the knife? Surely not use it as a weapon. What had she been thinking? And where did she think the two of them would go? What would they do?

She glanced at the envelope beside her on the nightstand, still upset and confused by what she'd found inside it. Nothing about the drug money Julio had stolen from Calderone. Nothing to help her.

She picked up the envelope. It still had some of Julio's blood dried into one corner. She felt nothing. Not a twinge at the sight of the blood, nor anything for the cold distant man who'd been her husband. What kind of woman was she? she wondered again. How could she feel nothing for the man who'd given her Elena?

She opened the envelope as if the contents might explode, slipping the papers out onto her lap, quietly, cautiously, not wanting to wake Elena, still stunned by what she'd found.

A passport and Texas driver's license tumbled out, the accusing eyes staring up at her from the photo on the license. The woman's name, it read, was Abby Diaz. Abby, like the name engraved on the silver heart-shaped locket. Abby Diaz, an FBI agent.

But what made Isabella's fingers tremble and her heart pound was that the woman looked like her.

She reached up to touch her face, running her fingers along the tiny scars left from her surgery. What had she looked like before the fire? She couldn't remember. Worse, why did she suspect she'd been made to look like this Abby Diaz?

She didn't want to think about that. Nor about the other papers she'd found in the envelope. She looked down at her daughter. Elena still had the locket clutched in her fist.

The sight tugged at Isabella's heart and concerned her more than she wanted to admit. Her daughter had cried until she'd been given the locket to hold.

The battered heart-shaped silver locket with a stranger's face inside it.

Then Isabella had awakened to find Elena on the phone and the envelope's contents on the floor beside her, the silver locket open and empty, the photo in Elena's small hand.

"Why did you call the number inside the envelope?" Isabella had demanded after she'd hurriedly hung up.

She didn't ask how the little girl had realized it was a phone number or how she'd known to make a call. Elena had taught herself to read at three. She was smart. Too smart, Julio used to say. Gifted. Precocious. Frightening even to Isabella sometimes. Her grandmother would have called Elena an Old Soul.

Elena had shown her the phone number and explained it was like ones Julio had called in the States. Isabella wondered who Julio had called.

"But why would you call *this* number?" she'd asked, growing more afraid for her daughter.

Elena had handed her the tiny photograph of the stranger from the locket. On the back was printed: "Love, Jake." When Elena had found the name Jake Cantrell in the envelope with a telephone number, she'd called it.

"Daddy will help us," Elena had declared stubbornly.

"*Julio* was your father," she'd said, "And he cannot help us."

Elena's lower lip had begun to tremble. Tears

welled in the child's eyes. "Daddy Jake will help us, though." She'd cried inconsolably until Isabella had put the picture back into the locket and given it to the child to hold again.

What disturbed her most was that Elena was convinced Jake Cantrell was her father. Why was that? Had Julio planted this seed? The same way the hospital surgeons might have been told to make Isabella look like another woman? A former FBI agent named Abby Diaz?

She felt sick now as she watched her daughter sleep. Elena expected some stranger to come and save them from Calderone's men.

But what the child didn't know was that if Jake Cantrell found them, it wouldn't be to save them. In the envelope, Isabella had found evidence that former FBI agent Jake Cantrell had set up his partner Abby Diaz to die in a drug raid six years ago. What scared her was that she looked enough like this woman that he might think she *was* Abby Diaz.

Isabella now feared that Elena's call for help had only given away their location and set an even more dangerous man after them.

Chapter Two

Everything from the wedding reception had been cleared away by the time Jake returned. The ranch house felt cool and dark and blessedly normal again. He regretted that he hadn't got to tell Brady goodbye before he took off on his honeymoon, but he knew Brady would understand.

He could hear Rosa and Slim in the kitchen, Slim trying to flatter the short, round, good-natured cook, but Rosa resisting the crusty old ranch hand's charm to the clatter of dishes and Mexican music on the radio.

He breathed it in, wishing he could get back some of the tranquillity he'd found over the last five years here at the Smoking Barrel. Usually riding his horse Majesty under the vast Texas sky brought him some peace. But not tonight.

He couldn't get the call off his mind. Still, he felt a little better after his long ride and regretted snapping at Penny earlier when she'd followed him down to the stables. She'd only been concerned, but he'd wanted to be alone. He'd felt like a powder keg ready to blow and needed to feel the wind in his face and a good fast horse beneath him.

Hat in hand, he now tapped lightly at Penny's door, hoping to catch her before she went down to the meeting.

She opened her door and looked surprised, the air around her sweet with the scent of perfume, her hair pulled up into a style he'd never seen on her before and a hairbrush in her hand. No, not surprised. Embarrassed to be caught primping. He wondered if the carefully applied makeup and new hairdo had something to do with the date he'd heard discussed over coffee this morning in the kitchen.

"These are for you," he said, drawing the fistful of wildflowers he'd picked from behind his back. They seemed too small a gesture, but her eyes lit at the sight of them and her face softened as she gazed up at him.

"You didn't have to do this," she said, too much understanding in her voice.

The last thing he wanted was sympathy right now. He wanted even less to discuss the call.

"I'm just sorry I barked at you in the stables before," he said, turning away quickly.

Before she could reply, he walked away. Downstairs, he took the hidden elevator to the basement, to find the three men already waiting for him. He realized Penny wouldn't be joining them. Cody and Rafe were discussing the recent cattle-rustling and new evidence that someone had been camping on the ranch. For once, the young and cocky Rafael Alvarez wasn't clowning around, but then Penny wasn't here. Half Spanish, half Irish, Rafe had a way with women and he loved to tease Penny mercilessly.

Cody Gannon, a former rodeo bronc rider and the youngest of the bunch, was insisting what should be done about the rustling. Mitchell Forbes seemed only to listen at the head of the table.

Wondering why a meeting had been called, especially without Penny present, Jake took his place, his gaze on Mitchell. The older man didn't look sixty-five, not even with his head of white hair. The ex-Texas Ranger and Vietnam vet owned the Smoking Barrel, a pretty impressive spread, even by Texas standards. On the surface, the widower seemed exactly what he was, a wealthy rancher.

Few people knew that the ranch was headquarters for Mitchell's ragtag group of misfits known as the Texas Confidentials—an offshoot of the Federal Department of Public Safety. The confidentials were secret agents who handled cases that required a bit more sensitivity and stealth. When they weren't on assignment, they worked the huge ranch just like the cowboys they were.

Jake knew he'd been handpicked for the job by Mitchell. He'd just never understood why. But he was grateful. Not only had Mitchell given him something to do that mattered, he'd given him a home and a family.

"I think that covers it." Mitchell's deep voice

pulled Jake back from his thoughts. "We'll step up security and see what happens."

Jake realized he hadn't been paying attention. Cody and Rafe got to their feet to leave, arguing over whose turn it was to ride lookout tonight. Jake started to rise, but Mitchell motioned for him to wait.

Once they were alone, Mitchell studied the tip of his cigar, taking his time to light it with an elaborate silver lighter, then he turned the lighter in his hand. Over and over, as if he didn't know quite how to begin. That wasn't like Mitchell.

Nor was he supposed to be smoking. Maddie would throw a fit if she knew. Maddie Wells, a neighboring rancher, was in love with Mitchell. His health was one of the things they squabbled about. That, and why Mitchell hadn't gotten around to popping the question.

For Mitchell to be smoking again— Jake watched him through a haze of cigar smoke, his earlier anxiety growing with each passing moment.

"Penny told me about the call from the little girl," Mitchell said at last.

Jake felt a wave of annoyance. Nothing that happened on the ranch escaped Mitchell's attention. Penny saw to that. "It was just a prank call. Penny shouldn't have worried you with it."

Mitchell studied him, the lighter suddenly motionless. "Jake, I got a call from Frank Jordan, over at the FBI. I believe you worked for him when you were with the Bureau."

Jake nodded warily.

"Julio Montenegro, a high-ranking distributor for Tomaso Calderone, has been killed. His wife and child are missing, along with a very large amount of Calderone's drug money. The FBI wants us to find the woman and child before Calderone's men do. Frank asked for you."

Jake stared at his boss in disbelief. For the last six years he'd wanted nothing more than to nail Calderone, but it had been Mitchell who refused to give him any assignment that had anything to do with the drug lord.

"Excuse me?" he said now, getting to his feet. "You're giving *me* this assignment? After all the years of telling me to forget what happened, to forget Calderone?"

Mitchell started to speak but Jake cut him off.

"Now, just because Frank asks, you're going to let me go after the wife and child of Calderone's top Mexican distributor? Would you like to tell me just what the hell is *really* going on?" he demanded, angry and not sure exactly why. Maybe because he didn't want to dig up the past again. Not now. Not when he'd finally accepted what Mitchell had for years been trying to convince him of. Getting Calderone wouldn't bring Abby back.

"Sit down, Jake," Mitchell said quietly. He puffed on his cigar for a moment. Tension stretched as taut as a hangman's noose between them.

Slowly, Jake sat back down. "Dammit, Mitchell, why now?"

"Jake, I've always told you that personal vendettas have no place in this business. That hasn't changed."

"If you think I can go into this and not be part of taking down Calderone—"

"This isn't *about* Calderone," Mitchell snapped. "This woman, Julio Montenegro's wife…Frank has reason to believe she might be Abby Diaz."

The words dropped into the quiet room like boulders. He was too stunned to breathe, let alone speak.

"Abby is dead," he whispered at last. He ought to know. He'd been one of the six-member FBI team that had gone into that building on a routine investigation, not knowing Tomaso Calderone was waiting for them. They'd walked into the trap and Abby had died in the explosion and fire that followed, along with two other FBI agents.

Mitchell took a puff on his cigar and continued as if Jake hadn't spoken. "Julio Montenegro recently contacted the FBI with a deal. He said he had proof that Abby Diaz was alive. He had rescued her from the fire that night. She was burned, but survived."

"No." Jake shook his head adamantly. "I saw her body after the fire."

"You saw *a* body. What if the charred remains found after the explosion weren't Abby's? Julio claims the body was that of woman who worked for him. Three bodies were found in that fire. We just assumed the female was Abby."

"Abby, Buster McNorton and Dell Harper," Jake

said, more to himself, than Mitchell. He could never forget.

"As we understand it, Julio kept Abby under wraps, hiding her as his wife in the small town where he lived in Mexico, until he was ready to make a deal. That deal was a trade. The FBI would help him get citizenship and into a witness-protection program in the States in exchange for FBI agent Abby Diaz."

"Why would he keep her *six* years?"

"Maybe he needed time to build himself a nest egg," Mitchell suggested. "He must have gotten greedy, though, and finally got caught."

He shook his head. "This woman can't possibly be Abby."

"Jake, if there is any chance that Abby might still be alive, you owe it to yourself to find out. Frank has already ordered that the body in Abby Diaz's grave be exhumed for identification."

He swore, pulling off his Stetson to rake a hand through this hair. "Dammit, Mitchell, I don't want this. I don't want Abby dug up. I don't want—" Cold fury filled him. "I don't want to relive Abby's death all over again. Nor do I want to do Frank's bidding for him. This feels like a trap. Or something Frank dreamed up to advance his career."

Mitchell puffed on the cigar for a moment, studying him. "They knew about the two of you."

Jake's gaze jerked up. He didn't have to ask who knew.

"They've always known."

Jake wanted to laugh. He and Abby had thought they were being so discreet. Hell, they were FBI agents, trained in deception. But it seemed they hadn't fooled anyone. Especially the people they worked for.

"Because of the affair you had—"

"It was a hell of a lot more than an affair," Jake snapped.

"—Frank wants you on this case. As her former FBI partner and lover, you are the one person who'll know whether or not this Isabella Montenegro is Abby Diaz or an imposter."

"Of course she's an imposter. I can tell you that without even seeing her."

"Jake, we have confirmation that Isabella Montenegro *was* burned in a fire and had to have plastic surgery. She's the right size, about the right age—"

"Come on, Mitchell. You aren't buying into this, are you? Someone wants me to think Abby is alive, that this is my...kid."

He'd actually believed that no one had known about Abby's pregnancy. But obviously someone had. And now they were trying to use it against him.

"It explains the fake phone call from the little girl. Don't you think if Abby were alive she'd have gotten in touch with me?"

His boss worried the lighter in his hand like a stone for a moment before he spoke. "Abby might have defected."

"Bull," Jake growled, getting to his feet again. "You didn't know her. You don't know what we had together. We were getting married. Dammit, Mitchell, we were going to have a baby.'' The words were out before he could call them back.

Mitchell nodded and frowned. ''That's what I was afraid of. Jake, this child with Isabella Montenegro, she's about five years old and—''

''No, dammit. If Abby *was* alive, she'd have contacted me,'' he said adamantly. ''Especially if she'd given birth to our baby.''

''She might have reason to believe you betrayed her,'' Mitchell said, the words seeming to come hard to him.

Jake looked at the man, speechless.

''Abby might believe you set her up to die in that explosion,'' his boss said. ''She might have been given some sort of evidence—''

''No!'' Jake cried. ''She'd have never taken the word of a man like Calderone.''

''What if the evidence came from the FBI?''

Jake stared at him. ''What are you saying?''

''Part of the deal with Julio was proof not only that Isabella Montenegro was Abby, but that she'd been the target the night of the explosion. Julio said he knew who'd tried to kill her and why. According to Frank, that evidence points to you.''

''You don't really believe—''

''It doesn't matter what I believe,'' Mitchell said, cutting him off. ''The point is, this woman might believe that you're a killer. A man who set up his partner and lover six years ago to die. That could explain why, if she *is* Abby, she didn't contact you.''

''That's crazy,'' Jake said. Abby was the target? It didn't make any sense. Two other agents had died that night as well and another was injured. ''Why? Why would someone want to kill Abby?''

Mitchell squinted through the cigar smoke. ''Maybe only Abby knows that.''

He shook his head. ''Wait a minute. If Frank really believes that I was the one who set up Abby, then why would he want me on this case?''

''Frank doesn't believe you had anything to do with Abby Diaz's death. Or alleged death. You're the obvious person to send. Like I said, you, of all people, will know if this woman is Abby.''

Mitchell slid a sheet of paper across the desk.

Jake watched him, his mouth suddenly dry.

''This is the faxed photo Julio sent Frank,'' Mitchell said. ''It's the Montenegro child and her mother. I think you'd better take a look, Jake.''

The black and white copy of the photograph was blurry, the resolution poor and the paper even worse. But Jake felt his heart lurch, his breath catching in his throat, the pain sharp and bright, blinding.

He stared down at the woman. Frank was right. Isabella Montenegro looked enough like Abby Diaz to make him ache. But that was the point, wasn't it? To make him hurt. To make him doubt himself. To make him desperately want to believe Abby was alive.

But *was* it possible? Could this woman really be

Abby? Or an imposter, designed to draw him back into something he'd spent six years trying to forget?

He shifted his gaze from the woman to the child in the photograph. His pulse pounded just at the sight of the little girl. He felt his eyes burn, his heart slamming against his ribs. Oh God, could it be possible? He couldn't take his eyes from the child's face. There was something about her. So small, so sweet. And so scared. He could see it in her expression.

He crumpled the sheet of paper in his fist and closed his eyes, his throat tight, the pain unbearable. He told himself she wasn't his daughter, but she was someone's, and damned if he'd let whoever was behind this use an innocent child to get to him.

But he knew he was lying to himself. As much as he fought it, he wanted it to be true. He wanted Abby to be alive. He wanted their lost child more than he wanted life itself. And knew he wouldn't rest until he found out the truth. He just feared he was walking into a trap, one that even if it didn't get him killed, would destroy him.

"I'll understand if you don't want this case," Mitchell said softly.

Jake did laugh then. He opened his eyes and looked across the table at his boss, his friend, the man who'd saved him from his obsession to destroy Calderone, from his need to destroy himself. "You know damned well you couldn't keep me off this case now."

"Then you think there is a chance this woman is Abby?"

Jake shook his head, his words belying the battle going on inside him. "Abby is dead. The woman is an imposter. So is the kid. And I'll prove it."

Mitchell let out a long sigh. "I thought you might feel that way." He regarded Jake for a long moment, his gaze sad, worried. Then he continued as if this was just another assignment. "One of Calderone's henchmen is already on her trail. Ramon Hernandez."

Jake knew of Ramon. A crazy, ferret-faced man with a thirst for blood. Calderone's kind of man.

"Frank is hoping you can find her before Ramon does and keep her alive until you can turn her over to the FBI back in the States," Mitchell said.

Jake only nodded. He wasn't worried about finding Isabella Montenegro. After all, finding people was his specialty.

What worried him was what he'd do *when* he found her. He'd thought he'd buried the past, but one look at the woman in the photo brought it all back. He swore a silent oath. If this woman was part of a ploy to make him believe Abby Diaz was still alive, she would rue the day she ever laid eyes on him.

And if she was Abby?

He wouldn't let himself think about that now. He had to get to her and the kid before Calderone's men did.

Chapter Three

Isabella Montenegro cracked the curtains to peer out into the dirt street. This time of the morning the plaza was still empty, the sun barely peeking through the adobe buildings. A dog barked in the distance. Coyotes howled, the sound echoing from the hills surrounding the small Mexican town.

She closed the curtain and glanced back at Elena sitting, half-asleep, on the edge of the bed. Her daughter looked as worried as Isabella felt. They both knew that Calderone's men were out there and they couldn't keep evading them much longer.

So why keep running? Why not just give up now? They couldn't possibly get away from Calderone, one of the most powerful, influential men in Mexico. Not a woman and a child with very little money, no defenses— Other than the knife she'd taken from Julio's chest, she reminded herself.

She shuddered at the thought. What *had* she been thinking?

And now she had not only Calderone and his men after her but possibly Jake Cantrell and the FBI.

That all-too-familiar feeling of defenselessness threatened to paralyze her. She ached from it and the fear. Not for herself but Elena. She had to protect her daughter. But how?

She had no idea. Yesterday, she'd felt as if she'd been on automatic pilot. Not thinking. Just moving. She hadn't taken Julio's car. Too conspicuous. Instead she'd stopped the first bus she'd seen and boarded, having no idea where she was headed. Did it matter?

The bus had been going northwest, along the U.S. border. She realized that she was headed for the States and that was where she wanted to go. She wasn't sure how she'd get the two of them across the border, but she knew that once they were across, it might be the one place she could escape Tomaso Calderone.

She and Elena wouldn't last long in Mexico. Not with Calderone's connections. She tried not to think past getting to the border, because she feared they'd never get that far.

Right now Ramon and the rest were probably outside waiting for her to open the door of the motel room knowing they had her trapped. No reason not to wait and take her peacefully. Quietly. Calderone would prefer that they not cause a commotion if possible. Not that anyone would help a strange woman and her child. Especially if told she had run away from her husband. From her responsibilities. Isn't that what had happened the last time?

But what could she do?

She looked around the motel room. It was small, with a makeshift kitchenette complete with cockroaches and beat-up cookware. She opened the cupboards, searching for something, she had no idea what. Just something to buy them a little time. Enough time to escape again. To be free just a little longer.

FINDING ISABELLA MONTENEGRO and her daughter had been child's play for Jake. Penny had traced the call from the kid to a rundown Mexican motel southeast of Del Rio, Texas. He figured she'd head for the States and try to cross the border at Piedras Negras, since that was the direction she was headed and it was closer than Ciudad Acuna across from Del Rio.

But he also knew that Calderone's men would figure the same thing. That's why he decided following Ramon Hernandez and his pack of *javelinas* would be the easiest, fastest way to get to Montenegro and the kid.

That was how he'd found himself in a tiny Mexican town about seventy miles from the border, watching Ramon's men wait for the sun to come up and Isabella and Elena Montenegro to come out of a dilapidated motel.

The narrow, one-story strip of five motel rooms faced the square and the church. Jake spotted two of Ramon's men hiding behind the rock wall of the church, another behind the motel. The men didn't look too concerned. It seemed pretty obvious that Isabella and her daughter would be coming out at some point and the men would be waiting.

A desert-dust-colored van was parked behind the church, the driver dozing. Ramon was down the street at the cantina having breakfast.

Jake had taken a room in the aging hotel. His window looked out over the square. He had a view of the church, the motel and the cantina. At this distance, he'd be able to take out Ramon's men easily—and Ramon as well, if it came to that. Then, by way of the balcony and fire escape directly outside his hotel-room window, he could grab the woman and kid.

He preferred not to kill Ramon and his men if possible but no matter what he did, he knew Calderone would hear about it and set an army of men after him. He just hoped to get out of Mexico before they caught up to him. But he wasn't going without the woman and kid.

Like Ramon's men, he waited without much concern. He'd checked out the small town and had convinced himself he hadn't walked into a trap. If it'd been a trap, Ramon's men would be wired with a bad case of the jitters, looking around anxiously, worried about the former FBI agent.

Instead, they seemed half-asleep and bored. They probably were. How hard could it be to catch a woman and a little kid?

He looked over the desert-hued adobe buildings, the sun grazing the tile rooftops, wondering if his instincts were trustworthy when it came to Calderone. He didn't want to end up like Daniel Austin, the Texas Confidential agent who was missing and presumed dead. Daniel probably hadn't thought he was walking into a trap, either. Nor had Abby.

Jake was thinking how Abby Diaz would have been too smart though to get caught in a motel like the one below his window. Nor would she have slept in this late with killers after her. The sun crested, bathing the dusty little town in gold.

He was thinking how Isabella Montenegro might have been made to look like Abby, but she couldn't be made to think like her, when suddenly, the pace picked up.

No more sleepy little Mexican town. No dozing, waiting for something to happen. In a matter of seconds, the motel-room doors began to fly open followed by loud curses as patrons stumbled out into the square.

Jake stared down at the commotion. Smoke rolled out of the doors of the rooms as if the entire motel was on fire.

He let out a curse, staring in disbelief as he came fully awake himself. Four of the five motel-room doors stood open, smoke pouring out. Couples stood in skimpy clothing or nothing at all, coughing and cursing, several of the men trying to hide their faces.

The motel was a brothel!

The noisy excitement brought onlookers from the

cantina and the church and the motel office. Ramon
Hernandez was one of the people who rushed out
into the square. And the man he'd had watching the
back of the motel ran around to see what was happening, as well.

Instantly, Jake saw that he had two big problems.
Ramon's men had blended in with the small crowd
gathering outside the motel. Shooting into this
bunch was out of the question. So was getting to
Isabella Montenegro and the kid without having to
confront Ramon and his men. The odds had suddenly changed.

The second problem was that Isabella and Elena
Montenegro weren't among the guests who'd tumbled out of the rooms. In fact, only the one motel-
room door was still closed and he could see smoke
curling from around its edges.

Where there is smoke there's—

He swore again and dove for the balcony and fire
escape. Either Isabella and the kid were still in the
motel room, dying of smoke inhalation or—

He rounded the back corner of the motel in time
to see a woman and a small child scurrying down
the alley, their heads draped with wet bath towels
like veils, smoke trailing after them.

As he passed the small open bathroom window
that the pair had just come out of, he realized he
hadn't given the woman enough credit. He shook
his head as he took off after her. Who *was* this
woman?

ISABELLA HAD FOUND the flammable kitchen cleaner under the sink. Her gaze had leapt to the bathroom window, then to the metal grate in the ceiling. Standing on the night table with a kitchen knife, she'd been able to pry the grate open. Sure enough, it was an air vent and she suspected it ran the length of the motel. At least she hoped so.

She climbed down and, taking the assortment of threadbare towels from the bathroom, she soaked all but the two largest and thickest with the cheap cleaning fluid. From beside the two-burner gas stove, she'd taken the box of matches and a candle she'd found next to the stove.

"I'm going to need your help," she'd said to her daughter.

Elena had nodded solemnly and looked up at the open metal grate as if she already knew what her mother needed her to do.

JAKE FOUND the discarded wet towels still reeking of smoke a few blocks from the motel.

But just when he was starting to think Isabella might not be as dumb as he'd first thought, she disappointed him. She made a serious mistake. She tried to flag down a bus.

Didn't she realize Ramon's men would stop and search the bus as soon as they realized she wasn't in the motel room? Apparently not. Either that, or the bus was the best plan she could come up with on short notice.

He wondered how she'd gotten this far as he

watched her from a distance, debating what to do. He didn't have to debate long.

The roar of an engine preceded the dust-colored van he'd seen parked behind the church earlier. One of Ramon's men was driving, another riding shotgun. Jake guessed the others were in the back. He wondered where Ramon was.

He looked back at the bus and the two figures running to catch up with the slowing vehicle. Dust churned up under the wheels, the tiny sun-soaked particles sparkling against the desolate background.

Jake swore as the van careened around the corner, headed straight for him and the bus. Isabella Montenegro and the kid had just run out of luck.

He lifted the rifle from under the serape he wore and, taking careful aim, squeezed off a shot. Boom. The right front tire blew. The van began to rock and reel out of control. One of the men hurled himself out the passenger side of the van just before it hit a low rock wall with a resounding crash. Steam billowed up from the badly crumpled front end and the engine died with a final groan.

Jake turned. The bus had stopped, the door open. But Isabella and the child were no longer next to it. Had she foolishly gotten in, thinking there was safety in numbers? Surely not.

Off to his right, he caught a glimpse of movement and saw a woman running with a child in her arms. He had to give the woman her due. She could move flat-out when she had to.

He ducked into an alley. He'd cut her off and get

her to hell out of this town before she got herself
and the kid killed. Or worse, got him killed as well.

ISABELLA ROUNDED a corner at a run, the sound of
the gunshots and the crash still ringing in her ears,
and skidded to a stop at the sight of the man blocking the alley.

He stood in the middle of the narrow alleyway,
boots apart, arms at his side, just yards from her. He
wore a serape. She could make out enough of the
short-barreled rifle's shape under the thick woven
cloth to know he was armed. She knew he was dangerous because she recognized him.

He wore a hat pulled down low. It shaded his
face, as did the sunless alley. But she didn't need to
see his face clearly to know who he was.

Right now, he looked like one of those gunfighter
heroes from an old spaghetti western. But she didn't
fool herself that this man was any kind of hero.

From the instant she saw him, it happened within
seconds. She stopped running and shot a look over
her shoulder. She could hear curses and running
footfalls and knew Calderone's men were close behind her.

She hugged Elena to her and swung her gaze back
to the man blocking the alley. FBI agent Jake Cantrell.

He hadn't moved, but he looked like he could in
an instant. And would. She heard Calderone's men,
close now. Any moment they'd come around the

corner of the building but suddenly they seemed less dangerous than the man facing her.

She started to turn and run back toward Calderone's men, but didn't get two strides before strong fingers closed over her arm and jerked her and Elena into a recessed doorway.

"Don't make a sound," Jake Cantrell warned as he flattened them against the wall with his body.

She could feel the solid steel of the rifle barrel pressed against one breast, the business end tucked up under her chin, cold and deadly. *"Silencio,"* she whispered to Elena.

She couldn't see Jake's face because of the way he had her pinned to the wall with his body and his weapon. But she could feel the coarse fabric of the serape against her cheek and the stark incongruity of the cold rifle barrel and the warmth where his body pressed against hers. She could also smell him. Dust. Sweat. Cedar. Soap. And an undentifiable dangerous male scent that filled her senses like an admonition.

The running footfalls stopped at the mouth of the alley. She could hear just enough of the hurried discussion among Calderone's men to know that they were desperate to find her and Elena. Ramon was furious, and if they came back without the woman and child—

Jake lifted her chin a little with the end of the rifle barrel.

Her fear made enough room for a pulse of anger. Why did he feel he had to threaten her further? Wasn't holding her at gunpoint sufficient? Holding her against a rough rock wall with his body *and* his weapon?

But she concealed the anger quickly, just as she'd learned to do with Julio.

Calderone's men moved on, running again, the sound of their retreat finally drowned out by the pounding of her heart and the terror and repressed rage thrumming through her bloodstream.

Jake Cantrell had them now. From the frying pan into the fire. Calderone's men had frightened her, but nothing like this cold, calculating man. A man who'd betrayed his partner. His country. A man who had no mercy. No honor.

The anger tried to surface again, but she held it at bay. How wonderful it would have been to let it out. Like releasing a wild beast that had been caged too long. To finally not feel defenseless.

He leaned back a little as if to listen, his body easing off hers and Elena's, but the rifle barrel still against her throat, his body still hard and unyielding.

She let her gaze rise to his face, getting her first good look at him.

She let out a gasp, feeling as if she'd been struck. It was the same visage as the one in the locket. But it wasn't his face that turned her blood to ice water, leaving her shocked and scared to her very bones.

It was his eyes.

He shifted his gaze to hers. Her heart thundered in her ears and her mouth went dry as she looked into the deep green depths of Jake Cantrell's eyes. The most unusual green she'd ever seen. But not unfamiliar. Dear God, no.

Chapter Four

Jake felt her gaze and looked down into the woman's face. Shock ricocheted through him. Stunned, he stared at her, his heart flopping like a fish inside his chest.

In the faxed photo, she'd resembled Abby Diaz enough to make him hurt. But now, he could clearly see the dissimilarities. The not-so-subtle differences. Differences that should have quickly convinced him the woman wasn't Abby Diaz.

Yet when he looked into her dark eyes he felt a jolt that shocked him to his soul. Something intimately familiar. Abby. My God, she *was* alive.

Her name came to his lips, his arms ached to hold her to him while his heart surged with joy. For just an instant, Abby Diaz was alive again and standing before him. And for that instant, he was fooled.

Then he saw something he should have seen immediately. She stared back at him with a cold blankness. She didn't know him!

He searched her gaze. Nothing. No reaction. No lover's affirmation. Nothing but fear.

He groaned inwardly. He hadn't realized how badly he'd wanted her to be Abby. Or how much it hurt that she wasn't. He'd even thought he saw something in this woman, felt something.

Slowly, he touched his fingers to her face, the lump in his throat making it impossible to speak. He jerked back, the tiny shock of electricity startling him. What a fool he was. It was nothing more than dry-wind static, something common in his part of Texas. But for just an instant, he'd thought it was something more.

He quickly brushed her long, dark, luxurious hair back from her cheek—and saw the tiny tell-tale scars. How much more proof did he need that she wasn't Abby?

And yet he gazed deep into her dark eyes again. Still hoping. But he saw nothing, no intimate connection. No hint of the woman he'd known. He could see now that she lacked Abby's fire. That irresistible aura of excitement that made the air around her crackle. That made his body ache and his skin feverish for her touch.

He'd been wrong. This woman wasn't Abby Diaz.

Still she held just enough resemblance to Abby to make him ache. Whoever was behind this had picked the perfect woman for the deception. She was about Abby's height. Five-four. And she had that same slight build. The same womanly curves.

But her face was different in ways he couldn't

quite define. She had the same wide, exotic dark eyes, the high cheekbones, the full, bow-shaped, sensuous mouth. The surgeons had done an incredible job, but they hadn't been able to make her look like his Abby. Not entirely.

He shook his head and flashed her a bitter smile. "If I didn't know better, I might think you really were Abby Diaz."

"I am Isabella Montenegro."

Her voice lacked Abby's spirit and fire and yet he thought he heard Abby in it. Her gaze met his for only an instant, then the dark lashes quickly dropped, the movement submissive, yielding. Nothing like Abby.

He yearned to see Abby's passion flare in those eyes. Anger. Defiance. Pride. Desire. All the things that were missing from this woman. Mostly he ached to see the passion that had smoldered in the depths of Abby's dark eyes. Passion that could ignite in an instant and set his loins on fire with just a glare.

When the woman lifted her gaze again, it held no spark. Only surrender. He felt a wave of regret. Of guilt, all over again, for his loss.

"What do you want with us?" she asked in a small, meek voice.

He shifted his gaze to the child. A curtain of thick black hair hid her face as she ducked her head shyly into her mother's shoulder. If this woman really was her mother.

"Come on," he said, motioning with the rifle before taking the woman's arm again. "I'm getting you out of here." He'd expected her to at least ask where he was taking her, but she didn't. She came without even a second's resistance. Without even a word of argument or question. Nothing like Abby.

He smiled bitterly again. She might resemble Abby, but she damned sure didn't act like her. Abby had always given him a run for his money. God, how he missed her. He felt sorry for this woman. She was out of her league.

He spotted Calderone's men about to search a passing motor home and quickly ushered Isabella and Elena in the other direction, back toward the vehicle he had waiting. The little girl ran along side her mother, her hand in the woman's. Neither turned to look back, to see if he was still there. They were obviously used to following orders. It made him wonder who they were and how their lives had reached this point.

He walked with the rifle in his hands but hidden under the serape, expecting an ambush, planning for it, almost welcoming it. A release for the anger building like a time bomb inside him. Who had cooked up this charade? Why? Not that it mattered. He swore to himself: he'd find out who was behind it and make them regret it.

The nondescript club-cab Ford pickup was parked on the far edge of town. It had a small camper shell on the back, a sliding window between the two, the opening large enough to crawl through, Mexican plates on the bumpers and a handmade sign on the side that read Umberto's Produce with a Nuevo Laredo phone number. The kind of pickup that would get little notice in this part of Mexico.

He'd thrown a mattress in the back, a blanket and a cooler with food and water, along with several large boxes of produce that hid everything else.

The woman stopped only long enough to pick up the little girl and the worn rag doll she'd dropped. Behind them, Jake heard gunfire and voices raised in anger. He kept moving, the woman in front of him, the child in her arms.

When they finally reached the truck, he put down the tailgate, moved the produce and motioned for the two to get in. For the first time, he noticed how exhausted the woman looked. The child had fallen asleep in her arms and Isabella looked as if only determination kept her standing. He figured she hadn't gotten much more sleep last night than he had.

Was it possible she was only a pawn in this?

He slipped the rifle into the built-in sling inside his serape and reached for the little girl.

The woman stepped back, hugging the napping child to her. Their gazes met and he saw her distrust, her fear. She didn't want to hand over the girl.

But she would. He saw that in her eyes as well. Because she knew she had no other choice. And she was a woman who accepted that.

He took Elena from her, keeping his eye on the woman. But he didn't have to worry about her making a run for it. Or trying anything. Even if it had been her nature to do something daring, he had the feeling that she wouldn't have done anything that jeopardized the girl's life. Nor would she leave the child behind, even to save herself.

Maybe Elena really *was* her daughter.

He laid the sleeping little girl on the mattress, her arm locked around her doll. Her hair fell away from her face. He'd been struck by the adorable innocence of her face in the fax photo, but in person, she was even more striking. She had a face like an angel. He'd never seen a more beautiful child.

The dark lashes fluttered against skin lighter than her mother's. Suddenly the eyes flashed open. He jerked back in shock. They were green. A deep, dark, emerald green. So like his own.

If Abby had lived— If their child had been a little girl— If she'd gotten her father's green eyes and her mother's coloring— Then she might have looked exactly like Elena Montenegro.

The pain was unbearable. The doubts were worse. Isn't this what the person behind this horrible deception had hoped for? That he'd be beguiled by this woman and her child? That he'd question whether she was Abby? Whether this beautiful little girl could be his? Or worse, wish it were so?

Anger swept over him. A grass fire of fury. Quick and deadly, all-encompassing.

"Get in," he ordered the woman, his mood explosive. It was all he could do not to grab her and shake the truth out of her. But the frightened look in her eyes stopped him.

She hurriedly climbed into the back of the pickup with the child, keeping her head down, her eyes averted from his.

He slid the boxes of produce over to hide the two of them from view through the narrow camper-shell window, then slammed the tailgate, closed the top, and stood for a moment, fighting for control. But his body shook like an oak in a gale, trembling from the inside out.

As he walked around to the driver's door of the truck, he slammed a fist into the side of the camper, making the pickup rock and denting the metal. No sound came within. But then, he hadn't expected one.

His hand ached, funneling some of his energy into physical pain rather than anger as he climbed into the pickup, slid in the key and started the engine. Prudence forced him to drive calmly, carefully, not to draw attention or suspicion by peeling out in the gravel or driving as fast and erratically as he'd have liked.

He felt as if he might explode if he didn't let off some of the pressure. But still he drove slowly. Out past the last adobe building. Out to the paved two-lane blacktop. He turned onto it and headed toward the Texas border. The road would fork fifteen miles ahead, the fork to the right going to the closest border crossing at Piedras Negras, the left continuing on north to Cuidad Acuna.

In his rearview mirror he watched a beater of an old car approaching fast. He slid down a little, keeping his face shaded by the hat and his itchy foot from flattening the gas pedal. The speedometer wavered at forty-five when the car swept up beside him. He could feel the gazes of whoever was inside, just as he could feel the trigger of the double-barreled shotgun he'd pulled onto his lap.

He pretended to pay no attention to the car beside him. He pretended to sing loudly with the radio, turning up the Texas station, blasting redneck noise.

After a moment, the car sped on past. Four men inside. Ramon and three of his goons. Jake wondered about the other men he'd seen guarding the motel. Where were they? Or had he taken them out in the van crash?

He watched the car disappear into the flat, tan desert horizon and kept the pickup at forty-five, letting it lumber along as he turned down the radio and listened to the soft murmur of voices behind him in the camper.

His Spanish was rusty. Abby had been fluent because of her Spanish grandmother, who'd raised her. She'd often reverted to Spanish when she was angry. He'd learned from her. But it had been a long time. He'd forgotten a lot.

"There's food and water in the cooler for you," he said over his shoulder.

After a moment's silence, the woman said, "Thank you."

The little girl said something in Spanish he didn't catch.

He turned up the radio and tried not to think about

them. Or what they might have been discussing. Unfortunately, he couldn't forget the trusting, fearless look on the little girl's face as she'd opened her big green eyes to meet his.

ISABELLA HAD HOPED Elena would fall back to sleep and let her alone so she could think. Her head ached from exhaustion and fear and confusion.

"I told you he would come to save us," Elena whispered in Spanish next to her.

She didn't have the heart to tell her daughter that Jake Cantrell hadn't necessarily saved them. More than likely they were just prisoners of a different man now. But still prisoners. Possibly worse. If what she'd read from the information in the envelope about the man was true, she and Elena could be in worse trouble than they had been before.

"I told you he was my daddy," Elena said, daring Isabella to disagree.

She didn't have the energy. Nor the conviction. There had been so little she'd understood about her marriage to Julio. Or her past, the one he'd filled in for her after the fire.

But the moment she'd looked into Jake Cantrell's eyes she'd known one clear truth.

Jake Cantrell was Elena's father.

She'd seen her daughter in the deep green of his eyes. But also in the familiar way his brow furrowed in a narrowed frown. In the intense intelligence she'd glimpsed behind all that green. In the small telltale mannerisms that genetics passed from one generation to the next.

Jake Cantrell was Elena's father.

But if she accepted that as truth, didn't she have to accept the rest as well? That she was Abby Diaz. Former FBI agent. Former partner and lover of Jake Cantrell.

That was where her mind balked. She had given birth to Elena, hadn't she? Wouldn't she have known if Elena wasn't her child? Felt something...wrong if the babies had somehow been switched at the hospital?

Her head ached and she knew she was trying to come up with an explanation other than the one staring her in the face.

She closed her eyes. Was it possible? Was she Abby Diaz?

She had to admit, she'd never believed brown-eyed Julio was Elena's father, any more than Elena had. It wasn't just Elena's green eyes, though they certainly did make Isabella suspicious. But Julio had told her that his brother, who'd died at birth, had had the same green eyes, that they ran in the family.

She'd suspected it was a lie and the reason her husband wanted nothing to do with her or their beautiful baby was because Elena was the result of an affair Isabella had had before the fire. It would have explained a lot. Especially Julio's coldness and her baby's green eyes.

But now she could no longer cling to that explanation any more than she could keep telling Elena that she was wrong, that the man in the front of the pickup wasn't her father.

"Go to sleep for a little while, *chica suena,*" she told Elena, and closed her eyes. Beside her, Elena began to sing the songs Isabella had taught her. Songs Isabella believed she remembered from her grandmother. But now she wasn't even sure that was true.

If she was this FBI agent Abby Diaz, then why didn't she feel it? She knew nothing about being an FBI agent. Why hadn't she remembered her training? Was it possible she'd been burned from an explosion during an FBI investigation in Texas instead of a house fire in Mexico?

And if there'd been any chance that she'd survived, why hadn't the FBI come looking for her years ago? Why hadn't they rescued her from Julio? Why hadn't Jake?

Her head ached and her stomach roiled. She didn't want to be Abby Diaz. Not a woman—if it was true—whom someone had tried to kill six years ago. Especially if that someone had been her partner, her lover, Jake Cantrell.

But the real question was, did he still want her dead?

Chapter Five

Isabella jerked awake as she felt the pickup slow. She reached for Elena, thankful and relieved when she found her daughter sleeping deeply beside her, her face peaceful, almost content. In the pickup's cab, the radio played softly. A country-and-western station out of Del Rio. How close were they to the border?

She pushed herself up into a sitting position. She couldn't have been asleep for long. Through the windshield she could see that the sun still hung low on the horizon, the cactus casting dark extended shadows.

With a start, she realized that Jake had turned off the paved highway onto a road that appeared to be little more than a dust trail. What was he planning to do with them? It crossed her mind that he might be looking for a place to kill them. No one would be the wiser out here in what was a very isolated part of the Mexican desert.

But did a man who planned to kill people offer

them food and water first? Did he rescue them from drug dealers and killers? Who knew with *this* man? If he'd set Abby Diaz up to die six years ago and if he thought there was even a chance she *was* Abby—

Feeling at a distinct disadvantage in the back of the pickup, she asked in English, "Do you mind if I come up front?"

He turned with a start as if he'd forgotten she was back there. Or wished he could. "Up to you," he said, but she was already slipping through the adjoining window and down onto the bench seat of the cab.

He didn't look over at her as she fastened her seat belt, but she saw his jaw tense and his hands grip the wheel tighter, his gaze fixed straight ahead on the ribbon of dirt road that wove through the cactus and scrub brush.

Covertly, she studied him from the corner of her eye, prodding her memory for some hint of recognition. Some glimmer of remembered emotion. If there was any chance this man had been her lover...

But she felt nothing. Except a tightrope of tension that stretched between them. Hers was from fear. But what about him? He seemed anxious. Why was that? Did he have something to fear from Abby Diaz?

It gave Isabella a chill to think that he might still have some reason to want his former lover dead— if she could believe what she'd read in the envelope. And why wouldn't she believe it? The evidence had been damning. Dates and receipts and phone transcripts. All compiled by the FBI. Proof that Jake Cantrell had tried to kill his partner.

But why, she wondered as she stared at the narrow dusty road and the desert that stretched to the horizon. What had Abby done to him to make him hate her so that he'd want her dead? The mother of his unborn child. Or had he known about the baby?

If only she could remember. Right now, she'd have been happy to remember that she was Isabella Montenegro. Her only one clear memory was her grandmother. Surely the wonderful grandmother she recalled had been real. Or had Julio made her up, the way he might have made up her past as Isabella Montenegro?

"Where are you taking us?" she asked quietly over the music playing on the radio, not wanting to wake Elena.

"The first phone booth I come to across the border," he said without looking at her. "The FBI will take it from there."

The FBI. Fear shot through her. Shouldn't she feel relieved? Why did the mere thought of him turning her and Elena over to the FBI spike her heart rate and make her sick and scared inside?

"What's in this for you?" he asked suddenly, reaching over to turn off the radio.

She could feel his gaze on her, hard, unforgiving. "I don't know what you mean."

His intent stare narrowed into a frown. He looked

like Elena when she was upset. "What were you promised for pretending to be Abby Diaz?"

"I'm not pretending to be anyone." *Except maybe Isabella Montenegro,* she thought. She heard herself repeating what Julio had told her about her past, how she was born in a small Mexican town, how her parents died when she was young and her grandmother raised her, how at sixteen she married Julio and finally, how her grandmother and Julio's mother and sister had perished in the fire that scarred her face and one shoulder.

"That's quite the story," he said, glancing over at her, his expression as unbelieving as his tone. "You certainly speak good English for a woman who's spent her whole life in Mexico. Are you also going to tell me that your husband didn't work for Tomaso Calderone? Or that you just happen to resemble an FBI agent named Abby Diaz who Calderone killed six years ago?"

He blamed Calderone for Abby's death? "My husband Julio worked for Señor Calderone," she admitted. How did she explain the way she'd lived the last six years? Trying hard to keep herself and Elena invisible when Julio and his men were around. "I cannot tell you why I resemble this woman, the FBI agent. I had nothing to do with my husband's dealings and until yesterday, I didn't even know of Abby Diaz's existence."

He held her gaze for a long moment, then looked back to his driving. "I suppose you also don't know where the money is that your husband stole from Calderone.''

"If I knew that, I would have tried to buy my freedom from my husband's employer.''

Jake laughed.

"What is it you find so amusing?'' she demanded in a flare of anger. She'd learned to control her emotions around Julio, especially her temper. So why was she letting it show with a man who was possibly even more dangerous?

"Buying your freedom would have been like trying to buy your soul back from the devil.'' He looked over at her. "Tell me something. This woman you described, this Isabella Montenegro, this woman you say you are, how is it she recognized me today in the alley? How do you know me?''

She didn't want to tell him about the manila envelope she'd found under Julio's body.

"Your picture was in the locket,'' said a small voice from the back of the truck in perfect English. Julio had forbidden Isabella to speak English under his roof, having long ago explained away why Isabella had awakened in the hospital six years ago, knowing both English and Spanish.

But she'd taught her bright daughter both languages in secret, warning the child never to speak English except to her and only when they were alone. She now regretted teaching her.

They both turned to see Elena sitting just behind them at the open window. Isabella wondered how long her daughter had been awake and how much she'd heard and understood.

"What locket?" he demanded.

Elena produced the heart-shaped piece of worn silver from her pocket and held it out as if it were a rare jewel.

He slammed on the brakes, bringing the pickup to a teeth-rattling stop, and snatched the locket from the child's hand.

His strong features seemed to dissolve in either pain or anger. Isabella couldn't tell which. He bent his head, running his thumb over the engraved letters of the locket, as dust settled around the pickup.

Then slowly, he opened the tiny silver heart.

His eyes closed as his fist closed over the locket. "Where did you get this?" he demanded, his voice breaking, as he swung around to face Elena.

"I gave it to her," Isabella said quickly, realizing she had no other choice now but to tell him about the envelope. If he looked into her bag, which he was bound to do before long, he'd find the envelope anyway.

"I found an envelope with the locket in it after my hus—after Julio was killed." Whether Julio had really been her husband or not, she refused to think of him in those terms. Not anymore.

He shot her a look. "How did your husband get it?"

"I don't know." She could see he didn't believe her. She couldn't really blame him. She knew so little. And yet she had much more than Jake's former lover's locket. She had her face. And her baby. No wonder he was so mistrustful.

"I want to see the envelope," he said.

She nodded and asked Elena to hand it to her.

Still sitting in the middle of the narrow dirt road, he dug through the contents, scanning the material inside, glancing at her periodically and finally letting out a curse when he found the evidence against him. He closed his eyes, the top of the envelope crushed in his large fist.

Then slowly his grip relaxed and he shoved everything but the locket back into the envelope and handed it to her.

"If you were Abby Diaz, it appears you would have something to fear from me," he said quietly, bitterness layered on top of anger.

She realized she'd been holding her breath. She let it out now and met his gaze. "But neither of us believes I am Abby Diaz."

He stared at her, his gaze probing hers. What was he looking for? His lost love? Or a hint of recognition on her part? She could give him neither.

"Even if you are who you say you are, the evidence in that envelope would make you think you couldn't trust me," he said carefully.

She said nothing. Trusting Jake Cantrell was the last thing she planned to do.

"For all I know, you aren't even Isabella Montenegro," he said after a moment. "Of course you have some indentification, some proof of who you are."

She nodded and pulled out the only piece of identification she had with a photo of her on it, taken after the fire. All other photos and identification of her prior to that had been burned in it.

"This is all you have?"

It did sound unbelievable, but not for a woman who never left the house except in the company of one of her husband's associates. "I've never had need for much identification."

"But you have Abby's passport, her driver's license, a copy of her birth certificate," he pointed out.

"I found them in the envelope only yesterday."

He nodded as he pocketed the locket.

Elena started to protest but Isabella stopped her with a warning look. "Play with your doll," she told Elena.

Jake got the truck moving again as Elena did as she was told and moved farther back. A few moments later, Isabella heard her talking softly to the rag doll.

The pickup rolled along for a few miles, the silence inside the cab heavy, laden with uncertainty.

She couldn't help thinking about the FBI. If Julio really had been working for them as the information in the envelope showed, how could the Bureau not have known about her and Elena? Why did she feel that at least someone in the FBI had known she was alive and kept it a secret?

"I don't understand why the FBI would be interested in Elena and me," she said.

He looked at her as if she were joking. "You've been living with one of Tomaso Calderone's top distributors, a man who knew enough of Calderone's business to steal millions from him."

Millions? Julio? She glanced out her side window at the passing desert, the sun already hot and stifling, even this early in the morning. Why did she find it impossible to believe? Because Julio had always been so fearful of Calderone, a man who would kill his own mother for money. No, Julio was not the kind of man who'd risk stealing that much money, knowing the consequences.

But if Calderone believed it, it would explain why his men were after her and Elena.

She jerked her gaze back around to Jake as another realization struck her. And Cantrell's next words made her feel he had read her thoughts.

"That's right, if you were Abby Diaz, the FBI would want to know what you've been doing the last six years, why you were living with Julio Montenegro as his wife, why you were pretending to be someone else and if you'd been helping Calderone. They'll also want to know where Julio hid the money."

She swallowed, her mouth suddenly dry. In other words, they'd think that she'd sold out her country and fellow agents. What were the chances they'd believe she couldn't remember even her name? About as much as Jake would if she told him about her loss of memory.

"But I'm not Abby Diaz," she said.

He gave her a humorless smile. "Lucky you."

She stared out at the dirt road ahead, trying to still her hammering heart. Even as Isabella Montenegro, the FBI wanted her. Planned to use her. To get Calderone? Or the missing drug money? Or both?

She realized Jake was looking at her.

"What are you afraid of?" he asked. "That the FBI can prove you're an imposter? That they'll arrest you for aiding and abetting a criminal?"

"What does *imposter* mean?" Elena asked from the back.

Isabella tried to hush her daughter, but Elena wasn't having any of it. "Imposter is—"

"It means fake, fraud," Jake said, his gaze on Isabella. "That's why the FBI has DNA tests, fingerprint comparisons, ways to expose the truth."

"Are you sure you can handle the truth?" she snapped, unable to hold back her anger. It was one thing to deny that she might be his former lover, but it was another to deny his child. What kind of man was he that he didn't acknowledge his own child? "Don't you already know? Can't you see what is right before your very own eyes?"

Elena crawled up into the front seat, into her lap. "My doll!" she cried as she realized she'd forgotten it in the back. Elena and the doll had been inseparable since Isabella had made it for her. "Get my Sweet Ana, Mommy. Please."

Jake felt as if he'd been kicked by a mule. "What is the doll's name?" he asked, telling himself he hadn't heard correctly.

"Sweet Ana," the woman said.

He could feel her gaze on him, feel the kid watching him too. *Sweet Ana.* "The kid come up with that?"

"Mommy named her. Mommy made her for me for Christmas when I was a baby."

He glanced at Elena, a little bowled over by her English and her confidence. She was smart. He could see that. Smarter than five, that was for sure. "How old are you now?"

"Four and three-quarters."

He smiled at that and her, and went back to his driving. Damn, she was a cute kid. All little girl.

"Why don't you want to be my daddy?"

"What?" He swung around to look at her.

Her eyes were big as CDs and that incredible all-too-familiar green, and she was looking at him with an expression that battered his heart with a club.

He shot Isabella a furious look over the top of the child's head. This was her doing.

"I'm not your father," he said more harshly than he'd intended. He thought the kid would burst into tears. He thought she'd at least leave him alone now.

"She's just a child. Don't hurt her because of how you feel about me," the woman whispered angrily.

How he felt about her? He stared at her, seeing Abby. Passion burning in her gaze. Even if it was only anger, it stirred something in him, confusing him, making him doubt everything, especially what he'd thought had happened six years ago.

"Why do you think you're not my father?" Elena asked, drawing his gaze again. She didn't sound upset, just curious, as if he were only trying to fool himself.

"Look, kid—" He met her gaze, feeling cursed with the same green eyes. She looked up at him, those eyes so filled with trust. With innocence. With longing for the father she wanted to see in him. "Why do you think I am?"

She smiled as if his question was just plain silly.

He pulled his gaze away from her, realizing he'd just driven off the road. Not that it mattered. This wasn't much of a road, anyway. This kid was rattling him more than he wanted to admit.

"Look," he said, "I don't know if I'm your father or not." He shot the woman a hostile glance, angry with her for putting him in this spot, angry with himself.

She just stared back at him as if he were the biggest fool on earth. He couldn't argue with that.

He told himself he didn't see Abby in those dark eyes. Didn't hear her in the woman's voice. Didn't sense her in the tension that arced between them. What had made him think this would be easy? An open-and-shut case. One look and he would know if she was Abby.

Elena smiled up at him and hugged the worn, homemade rag doll in her arms. Her Sweet Ana. "You are my daddy," she said with conviction, those green eyes gazing up at him with open affection. "You'll see."

Damn, he thought as he looked away. This woman already had him doubting himself enough, without seeing those Cantrell green eyes in this little girl. What the hell was wrong with him? He was letting a little kid con him. He was damned glad the gang from Texas Confidential wasn't here. Wouldn't they love this. He sped up the truck, anxious to turn these two over to the Feds.

"We're almost to the border," he said. "You'd better get your things together." He was grateful when they climbed into the back again. He concentrated on his driving, speculating on what might lie ahead at the border, rather than thinking about the woman and little girl in the back of his truck.

He stopped just outside of Cuidad Acuna and disposed of the Umberto's Produce signs, the produce, the mattress, his serape, instructing Isabella and Elena to get into the front again. He hid his weapons in the truck, changed the plates back to Texas ones, then climbed in again, unable to shake a bad feeling that he'd been led into a trap—just as he'd suspected.

The evidence in the envelope had been compiled by the FBI. So that meant that Frank knew about it. Damning evidence that made him question his own innocence. So why was he still walking around? Why wasn't he behind bars?

But the bigger question was, why had Frank chosen him for this job?

It made him nervous. Something wasn't right.

His original plan had involved help from the FBI

to get across the border with the woman and kid. But that was no longer necessary. Nor his first choice. The woman could use Abby's identification at the border. Her likeness to the photo was enough to convince any immigration officer. Not that they paid that much attention. An American and her child could easily cross the border. An American and her husband and child could cross even easier.

And right now, he didn't want to tip off the FBI. He had a bad feeling he couldn't trust Frank Jordan.

"Abby was born in Dallas," he said to the woman as they neared the border, taking the truck route through the industrial part of town. "For the moment, you're Abby Diaz." He looked over at her.

She nodded but said nothing, her gaze on the border town.

"Elena," he said, using the child's name for the first time. "If the border guard says anything to you, speak English."

"I understand," Elena said.

"Good," he said. Her smile made him ache. He turned back to his driving, watching his rearview mirror as well as the side streets and the town ahead, telling himself he'd better be ready for trouble. Like he already didn't have enough in the cab of the pickup.

He was counting on Ramon and his men going to the closest border crossing, some fifty miles away. Unless he missed his guess, they'd still be there, waiting, expecting the woman and child to take the fastest route to the States. He told himself Ramon wasn't smart enough nor did he have enough men to cover both border crossings.

Lost in those thoughts, Jake didn't see the man step out into the street in front of the pickup until it was almost too late. He hit his brakes. The truck skidded to a stop and died just inches from the man. As the man turned, Jake saw the pistol in his hand and realized belatedly that Ramon Hernandez was a lot smarter than he'd originally thought.

"Get down," Jake cried to Isabella as he shoved Elena to the floorboards.

But it was too late. Before he could get the truck started, Ramon put a round into the pickup's engine.

One of Ramon's armed thugs jerked open the passenger door and grabbed Isabella by the arm. As she struggled to fight him off, Elena screamed for Jake to help her. Jake slammed down the lock on his door as another man came around to his side of the truck.

"Put your head down," he yelled at Elena as he groped under the pickup seat for the semiautomatic he'd duct-taped there, wrestled it free and fired, dropping the man beside Isabella with two quick shots that reverberated through the cab like dual explosions.

The driver's-side window shattered behind him. Before he could turn, his door was jerked open and he was grabbed from behind in a half nelson, the man's free hand on Jake's pistol as he tried to wrestle it away.

The man was strong and had Jake pinned in the pickup in a position where he could do little to free himself. The arm at his throat was cutting off his air. He felt his fingers weakening on the weapon and heard Elena cry out something in Spanish to her mother. Darkness edged his vision as the pressure from the man's arm cut off his air.

He heard the shot, felt the arm around his neck loosen, the hand on his weapon release. The first shot was followed quickly by a second. The man behind him made a small grunt before he hit the ground with a lifeless thud. The third shot, which came within seconds of the other two, made a hollow sound as it punctured the windshield, driving a clean hole through the glass and instantly turning the glass around it into a thick white web.

Jake heard the sound of someone running, the roar of a large car engine and the screech of rubber as the sound of the engine died away.

Beside him, one of Ramon's men lay in a pool of blood, staring up, a neat little black hole between his eyes.

Jake swung around to look at Isabella as he gasped for breath, his throat on fire where the man had choked him.

She sat perfectly still, except for the trembling of the hand that held the pistol. A pistol she must have taken from the man he'd killed on her side of the truck. He looked quickly at Elena, still huddled on the floor.

"Are you all right, Elena?" he asked, his voice hoarse.

She lifted her face from her knees, her doll clutched to her thin chest, and nodded, eyes wide.

In the distance, he could hear the sound of police sirens. He knew he wasn't going anywhere in this truck and now, more than ever, he needed to get out of Mexico. "Come on," he said to Isabella.

She still hadn't moved. She seemed in shock. No more than he was, he thought.

"We have to get out of here," he said, touching her arm.

She stirred at his touch, her gaze settling on him for a moment, then quickly flicking to Elena. Tears welled in her eyes as she dropped the gun and reached for her daughter.

Jake shoved his pistol into the waist of his jeans, then took Elena from her mother's arms. "We're going to have to run. Are you up to it?" he asked Isabella.

She nodded and pulled her bag from the back. A second later she was out of the truck and running beside him down a side street.

He ran with Elena, her one small arm wrapped around his neck, the other around her Sweet Ana. As he wound through the narrow streets, he looked for a vehicle to steal, trying to ignore the voice in his head, the one that kept reminding him of the perfectly placed bullet hole and the only other woman he'd known who could shoot like that.

Abby Diaz.

Chapter Six

The red short-box Toyota pickup was almost too easy. It had Texas plates, was parked at the edge of the industrial area and was one vehicle he could hot-wire in less than a minute.

Jake would have much preferred something a little less flashy than bright red. But beggars couldn't be choosers.

However, when he got closer, he realized hot-wiring it wouldn't be necessary. Not only was the truck unlocked, the keys glittered in the ignition. He glanced around nervously. When things went too easily it made him nervous. When they went this smoothly, it scared the hell out of him.

Jake quickly ushered the woman and child into the front bench seat, worried either that the owner hadn't gone far and would return too soon or that he'd just walked into an ambush. He hurried around to the driver's side and slid behind the wheel. The truck started on his first try.

The Mexican town still dozed in the warm, early-morning sun. He drove toward the border, avoiding the part of town where he could still hear police sirens. Three minutes later, he pulled into the short line of commercial trucks and several cars at the border crossing, still looking over his shoulder. For Ramon. For the owner of the pickup. Afraid someone would stop them before they could reach the States.

The line moved as slow as mesquite honey. When their turn came, the border guard ambled over to Jake's side of the pickup and leaned down to peer at the three of them. He asked the standard questions. Were they American citizens, where they were born, what had they been doing in Mexico and had they purchased anything.

Jake wondered if Frank had alerted the border guards to watch out for him and his companions. That would be like Frank. If Frank had his way, he'd have Isabella and Elena in protective custody the moment they stepped on U.S. soil.

But the guard barely glanced at them or their drivers' licenses before he waved them on through.

Still, Jake found himself holding his breath as he drove into Texas. He watched the highway ahead and behind them, expecting—hell, that was just it. He didn't know *what* he expected.

Well, at least he was back in Texas. Home. He'd done what he'd been assigned to do. Find the woman and child, get them to the States. Now all he had to do was call Frank and have the Feds pick them up. Job done.

He glanced down at the speedometer and quickly lightened his foot on the gas pedal. *Don't be a fool, Cantrell. All you need to do is get picked up for speeding in a stolen vehicle.*

But he couldn't deny the need to put distance between them and Mexico. Or the unaccountable urge he felt to run.

The question was: run from what? He watched the highway. No Ramon. No nondescript car with occupants who looked like agents. He told himself he could relax now. He was back in Texas. Safe.

He looked over at the little girl, her face lit with excitement as she stood on the seat, staring ahead at the town of Del Rio. Then past her to her mother. The woman's eerie resemblance to Abby struck him like a blow—just as it always did. Now, though, after what he'd witnessed in Ciudad Acuna—

"That was some shot," he said.

Yes, it had been. She'd thought of little else since. "I can't believe I did that. It just happened so fast."

Her hands had stopped trembling but she was still shaking inside. She'd killed one man and would have killed the other one if he'd given her the chance.

Even now it didn't seem like her hand that had wrenched the pistol from the dead man's fingers and fired without hesitation. She didn't even know she knew how to shoot let alone could hit anything.

But she'd more than just hit something, hadn't she?

"I just pulled the trigger," she said, trying to convince herself as much as him. "Anyone could have hit such a large target at that close range." Was that true?

She dragged her gaze from the Texas town to look over at him, afraid of what she'd see.

He stared at her openly, suspicion in his gaze as he searched her face. She knew what he was looking for. Abby Diaz. He was beginning to suspect what she'd feared.

"You must have shot a pistol before," he said.

She noticed the careful way he chose his words. "Not that I can remember," she answered truthfully.

He nodded, eyeing her intently before turning back to his driving. "Lucky shot, for your first time."

She said nothing. She'd shot the man between his eyes. No hesitation. The pistol in her hands had felt almost...natural. She looked out her side window and watched the city of Del Rio rush past in a blur, remembering the look on the man's face, the shock when she'd turned the pistol on him and fired.

Dear God. She closed her eyes. Who was she? Certainly not Isabella Montenegro, housewife and mother, prisoner of Julio Montenegro in a loveless marriage.

She opened her eyes. Why couldn't she accept what had to be the truth?

She glanced over at Jake. A thought struck her, taking her breath away. She'd always wondered why she couldn't remember anything before the fire. At first she'd thought her loss of memory was due to the accident. But the doctors had told her it was psychosomatic, caused instead by trauma or repression due to possible shock. In other words, she'd blanked out the past because she couldn't face it.

Couldn't face that someone close to her, someone she'd trusted, maybe even loved, had betrayed her?

The thought sent a chill through her. If that were true, then Abby Diaz knew her killer. Knew him and trusted him. Just as she might have her lover. The father of her child. If Jake really was guilty, then wouldn't he now be afraid she'd identify him to the FBI?

If only she could remember. Dear God, what had happened six years ago?

She realized Jake hadn't stopped at a phone booth yet. Hadn't he said he was taking her to the first phone booth, calling the FBI and turning her and Elena over to the Feds?

But he seemed to be driving straight through Del Rio as if he had no intention of stopping. Her heart took off at a gallop. He'd been so anxious to wash his hands of her and Elena. What had changed?

Had he changed his mind because of what had happened in Ciudad Acuna? Did he suspect that she was Abby Diaz? Is that why he'd changed his plans?

Her pulse throbbed at her temple, the morning sun blinding. She pulled Elena closer, fear making her chest tighten, her mouth dry.

They passed another phone booth. "Are you going to call the FBI or take us to the nearest office?"

she asked, trying to keep the anxiety out of her voice.

"I'm not taking you to the FBI just yet," he said without looking at her.

Her heart thudded dully in her chest. She looked out at the small Texas town, fighting panic. Once they left these streets and were out in the open desert again— She leaned down and whispered into her daughter's ear. Elena whispered back.

"Elena has to go to the bathroom," she told Jake.

He glanced over at them, not looking happy about the prospect, then glanced at the gas gauge. "All right. We need gas, anyway. Can she hold it just a little longer? I'd really like to get to the other side of town."

She nodded and reached down to pick up her bag from the floor.

"But you'll have to make it quick," he added. "We have a long way to go." His gaze locked on hers, suspicious.

He didn't trust her. Not that he probably ever had. But now he'd be careful. Cautious. More watchful. And he'd changed his plans.

She could think of only one reason he'd decided not to take them to the FBI yet.

We have a long way to go. She hated to think where he might be planning to take her and Elena.

He stopped at a small, deserted gas station on the far edge of Del Rio. "Just a minute," he said as Isabella started to get out, her bag in one hand,

Elena's small hand in the other. He took the bag from her. "You won't need this, right?"

She looked up at him. Compliant was a look she'd perfected with Julio. "I just need a change of clothing for Elena and me. These clothes still reek of smoke."

He nodded, seemingly reassured as she pulled out what she needed, then she let him take the bag and put it behind the pickup seat.

She climbed out and, taking Elena's hand, walked toward the ladies' room. She heard his door open, heard him begin to fill the gas tank. She knew he was watching them. She knew she'd have to be careful. Just as she had been with Julio.

TEN MINUTES LATER, Jake saw her and the little girl come out of the ladies' room. The two of them made a striking pair and he couldn't deny the resemblance between mother and daughter. If he even considered that Elena might be his daughter, then—he caught the woman's eye. She quickly looked down at the child as the two advanced.

He didn't know what to think. What to believe. Right now he was just scared and not sure exactly what it was he feared the most.

A dust devil whirled across the pavement to shower the side of the nearly derelict building with Texas dust. He glanced at the road, unable to shake that uneasy feeling. But there was little traffic out this way and they had the gas station to themselves.

When he turned back, the woman and child were

almost to him. He finished filling the tank with unleaded and waited until she'd led Elena around to
the passenger side of the truck before he went in to
pay. In his pocket, he jingled the keys just to assure
himself he hadn't left them in the ignition. And he
kept an eye on the pair. Not that he thought the
woman was fool enough to take off on foot. Not
with the child.

While he paid the cashier, a teenage boy watching
a rerun on an old black-and-white TV, he had the
feeling of being observed. He looked out at the
pickup. Elena stood at the driver's-side window,
staring at him with an intensity that unnerved him.
He suddenly realized he couldn't see the woman.

Hurriedly, he took the change the teenager absently handed him, the TV still squawking in the
corner, and left the office, his anxiety growing with
each step he took toward the pickup.

She came around the front fender with a squeegee
in her hand and began to wash the windshield. He
almost laughed in relief and surprise. Someone had
certainly trained this woman well. Then he remembered the way she'd fired the gun and wondered just
how trained she really was.

"Here, let me do that," he said, going around to
the passenger side of the truck to where she
scrubbed enthusiastically at the bugs on the dirty
windshield.

She'd changed into a Mexican embroidered top
and jeans. The top billowed out, hiding her curves

as she worked. She turned to look at him, her gaze quickly dropping behind the veil of dark lashes.

He studied her a moment, wondering. One moment she was so passive, so subservient, a woman whose will had been broken. And the next? She was shooting a man between the eyes with a pistol as if it was the most normal thing in the world.

She handed him the squeegee, her fingers brushing against his. He was hit with that sudden unmistakable twinge again. The same one he'd felt the first time he'd seen her, the first time he'd touched her. And he had the most irresistible desire to pull her into his arms and kiss her. If he kissed her, he'd know. He felt certain of it. And wasn't that what was driving him crazy? Not knowing for sure?

Their bodies were so close that her scent filled his senses, reminding him of something rare and exotic. And…familiar.

The feel of the cold hard barrel of the pistol pressed into his ribs caught him completely by surprise. He blinked. Too shocked to comprehend what was happening for a moment. Where had she gotten a gun? He had his on him and—the other gun. What a fool. He'd just assumed when he hadn't seen her with the pistol she'd taken from Ramon's henchman that she'd left it in the produce truck. Dropped it like a hot potato.

He closed his eyes and groaned. What the hell was wrong with him? But he knew the answer to that as he opened them again and looked at the woman.

"The keys to the truck, please," she said.

He stared into her dark eyes and saw an intelligence that he'd somehow missed before. No, that she'd kept hidden, just as she'd hidden the anger and determination that now burned as bright as dazzling sunlight in her gaze.

"This is a mistake," he whispered, and felt the steel dig a little deeper into his flesh.

"The mistake will be yours if you don't give me the truck keys," she said calmly, her eyes locking with his.

The last thing he wanted to do was give her the keys to the pickup. But he realized she could kill him where he stood in an instant and from the look in her eyes, he didn't doubt she would. She probably believed the evidence in the envelope. Believed he was a killer.

Then she couldn't possibly be Abby Diaz. Abby would never have believed that he could hurt her—even if the information *had* come from the FBI.

"Easy," he said as he slowly reached into his pocket for the keys. He handed them to her, wondering, *now what?*

She produced a pair of handcuffs from the waistband of her jeans, cuffs that had been concealed under her billowing blouse. *His* handcuffs. The ones he'd unclipped from his belt and slipped under the seat of the pickup just before they'd reached the border.

She handed him the cuffs. "One on your right wrist, the other to the pump handle."

''You and the kid don't stand a chance on your own.''

''I'll take my chances. The cuffs, please.''

He glanced toward the gas-station office. The attendant was probably watching the TV he'd been glued to earlier. Not that the boy could see what was happening on this side of the pickup even if he'd bothered to look. No doubt that was the way she'd planned it. If only someone would stop for gas. But then he'd purposely chosen this rundown station because it *wasn't* busy.

He let out a curse as the pistol barrel pressed deeper into his flesh beneath his shirt, drawing his attention quickly back to the woman.

''The cuffs,'' she reminded him.

Completely gone was the passive female he'd originally thought he was taking to the FBI. This woman had a fireworks show of anger and pent-up aggression in her dark eyes.

And she had the pistol in the perfect spot to kill a man before he could make a move to save himself. Just luck, like the shot she'd fired between the man's eyes? *Right.*

He cursed himself for the fool he'd been as he snapped one cuff to his right wrist, the other to the gas pump. He'd underestimated her. Whoever the hell she was.

He met her gaze. She seemed to hesitate and in that instant, he felt something arc between them, strong and fierce and—this time no mistaking it—passionately familiar.

''Abby?'' he whispered.

And then the lights went out.

Chapter Seven

Ramon Hernandez was not having a good day. His half-finished breakfast hadn't agreed with his stomach, the van was demolished, and three of his men were dead and another two hurt too badly to be of much use.

He swore to himself as he stepped gingerly into the hot, cramped phone booth, watching his back. Outside, one of his remaining, least-injured men stood guard; little consolation, all things considered.

He quickly dialed the number, nervous, sick to his stomach and frightened. Who was the gringo with Isabella Montenegro? DEA? Or a drug dealer? He didn't like this added complication, whoever the man was, and wished he'd killed him when he'd had the chance.

A gust of wind whirled dirt against the weathered glass, making him jump. He mopped his brow, the slanted early-morning sun bearing down on the booth, making him feel like a target.

"We have a problem," he said when Tomaso Calderone came on the line.

"*You* have a problem," Calderone snapped.

Yeah. Well, Calderone didn't know the half of it. "Isabella Montenegro and her whelp pulled a fast one and got away, but someone is helping her."

"Who?"

"I don't know. A gringo. He grabbed her and the kid."

"Where were *you* when this happened?" Calderone demanded.

"Staking out the front of the motel," he lied quickly. "I had two men behind the motel." He wished. Who would have thought she'd set some sort of fire as a diversion and go out that tiny bathroom window? "The gringo killed three of my men, then shot out the tires on our van when we were in pursuit, destroying it." Lying came easy. It was probably his second best talent, lying on his feet. Killing was his first.

"I had to commandeer a car," he continued quickly, wincing at the sight of the large, older-model American car lounging like a lizard in the street. He wasn't about to tell his boss that he'd had the gringo in his sights and had foolishly killed his pickup instead. It was so hard to get good help these days.

"What did this man look like?" Calderone asked quietly.

Ramon described him.

"Why would *he* be interested in Julio's wife and

child?'' Calderone muttered almost to himself. "Listen to me, Ramon. This man is very dangerous. I want him. And I want my money. You do understand?''

"Si," he said, feeling sicker. Surely he'd heard wrong. "You don't want him...*alive?*"

"Oh, yes. I want them *all* alive."

Ramon swore silently. This would be very difficult and a waste of his true talents.

"What do you know of this woman and child?" Calderone asked.

Ramon shrugged to himself and looked out into the street. What did he know of Julio's life? Like Calderone, he lived farther south in Mexico. He had only seen the woman briefly and had paid little notice to her or the child with her.

"She looked like...a wife," he answered lamely.

"Mexican?''

"Si."

"I wonder...." Calderone mused.

"Who is this gringo?" Hernandez asked, a little concerned since he'd now be chasing him into the States.

"Jake Cantrell. He used to be an FBI agent."

"But he's not anymore," Ramon said, relieved he wouldn't be dealing with the FBI.

"He'll head for someplace he feels safe," Calderone said, as if still thinking out loud. "Let me make a call. Give me your number. I will get back to you when I know where he has gone."

Ramon hung up, wondering how Calderone knew

so much about this gringo. Had recognized him immediately from Ramon's description.

The phone rang a few minutes later. What Calderone told him more than surprised him. Maybe this wouldn't be so difficult after all. As long as he got the credit for bringing in Jake Cantrell, former FBI agent.

"Do not fail me, *amigo*," Calderone said after he'd promised to send him several more men. The line went dead.

As dead as Ramon Hernandez himself would be if he failed. The only good news was that the former FBI agent was traveling with a woman and child. That would hamper any man. And now Ramon would have help.

ISABELLA'S BODY trembled, her knuckles white on the steering wheel.

"You're scaring me, Mommy," Elena cried.

"I'm sorry, *chica suena,* I don't mean to scare you."

"But you hurt him," she cried, turning to stare out the back window at Jake on the ground beside the gas pump.

"He'll be fine," she assured her daughter. "He'll just have a headache when he wakes up." How did she know that? How did she know to hit him the way she had and not kill him?

She stared for a moment at her hands gripping the wheel as if they belonged to a stranger. She feared that they did.

Elena swung back around, tears glistening on her sweet face.

Isabella reached over to thumb the wetness from her daughter's cheeks. The child's lower lip trembled and big tears welled in her green eyes like pools of spring water. "He *is* my daddy."

"Yes," she agreed. "He is your father."

"Then why did you do that?" Elena demanded.

"Because I'm not sure we can trust him." He hadn't harmed her or Elena. But he'd changed his plans to turn them directly over to the FBI. Because he was afraid she really was Abby? Afraid she remembered that it had been Jake Cantrell who'd tried to kill her six years ago?

She thought of the way Jake had reacted to the locket. He'd appeared almost ready to break down with grief. A strange reaction for a man who'd tried to kill his lover.

She shook her head. She wasn't sure of anything at this point. Especially her reaction to him. That was why she wasn't taking any chances. But she couldn't shake off the memory of what had happened back at the gas pumps. That almost remembered feeling of…what? Passion?

Whatever it had been, it was gone again. And now she couldn't be sure what she'd felt. If anything.

"You are acting so…different," Elena said.

"I know, but I have to be strong right now. And you have to be strong. There are people who want to hurt us."

Elena wiped at a tear. "The people who killed Julio?"

"Yes. And others. I have to keep you safe, no matter what else I have to do. Do you understand?

The child nodded. "You always keep me safe."

Her eyes burned. "I have always tried."

"Where are we going?" Elena asked, looking out at the highway ahead.

Good question. As soon as Jake woke up, he'd either figure out a way to free himself or raise such a ruckus, the station attendant would hear him and call someone. Either way, it wouldn't be long before he'd be after them again. This time, with the help of the FBI, unless she missed her guess.

She'd have to ditch the pickup and get another means of transportation before she could leave Del Rio. How would she do that? Did she know how to hot-wire a car? She thought not. Nor did she expect to be as lucky as Jake had been in Ciudad Acuna.

She pulled up to a stop sign and rolled down her window, letting in the morning air, already hot although it wasn't even eight yet. In the distance, she heard a train's whistle.

JAKE WOKE with a start to find the gas station attendant standing over him, holding a dripping empty bucket and wearing a perplexed expression.

"How come you're handcuffed to my pump?" the boy asked.

For a moment, he couldn't remember. Or maybe

he just didn't want to. "My girlfriend and I had a little falling-out."

"Really?" the kid said. "You must have really ticked her off."

"Yeah." He sat up. His head ached, and unfortunately, the memory of what had happened came back in minute detail. He still couldn't believe it. Might not have, except for the bruised skin just below his ribs where she'd jabbed him hard with the gun, and the raised, painful lump on his head where she'd nailed him.

Nor could he forget what he'd seen in her eyes just before she'd hit him. He shook his head and groaned, his head aching from more than the blow as he stumbled to his feet.

Besides the headache and still being handcuffed to a gas pump, he was soaking wet from being doused with a bucket of cold water. But the water *had* done the trick. He glanced at his watch. He hadn't been out long. If he hurried—

"Do you have a cell phone?" The boy nodded. "Get it. And bring me a hacksaw, will ya?"

"AMTRAK'S SUNSET LIMITED from New Orleans pulls out of Del Rio, Texas headed for points west at 8:30 a.m. Sunday, Monday, Thursday and Saturday," the clerk said. It was Thursday.

She had only enough money to buy two coach seats as far as El Paso and just hoped that would be far enough.

"I'm hungry," Elena told her the minute they got on the train.

"As soon as we leave the station, I'll get you something to eat."

She'd gotten a window seat on the station side and pulled down the shade, leaving it open just enough that she could still see the platform. So far she hadn't spotted any of Calderone's men. Or Jake Cantrell. Not that she thought she would. He and the FBI would be looking for the red Toyota pickup, expecting her to still be driving it. But how long would it take them to find the truck parked in the junkyard down the road from the train station?

The train started to move. She leaned back, finally beginning to relax a little. Through the window, she watched the last of Del Rio sweep past. She looked for Jake's face, or Ramon's and the rest of Calderone's men, in the people they passed along the way. But she didn't see anyone who looked familiar.

"Let's get some breakfast," she told her daughter when Del Rio had disappeared entirely and only desert stretched to the horizon.

In the dining car, she ordered the Tucson Morning for Elena, two pancakes, butter and syrup, and the Sunrise Limited for herself, eggs and grits.

They ate in silence, Elena making short work of her pancakes and then finishing most of her mother's eggs and grits. Elena sulked. She'd finally found her father. Only to lose him again. Thanks to her.

When they'd finished breakfast, they went back to their seats and Elena fell asleep to the rocking of the train, while she stared out the window. Miles and miles of flat desert as far as the eye could see. The train clattered along and she had to admit at last, she wasn't the woman she'd believed she was for the last six years.

JAKE STILL HAD one person in the FBI he thought he could trust. He called Reese Ramsey, a man he'd trusted with his life more than a few times when they'd worked together as agents. Reese, true to form, didn't ask any questions, just listened until he'd finished.

"Two agents will bring you what you need in the next fifteen minutes," Reese said. "If you need anything else—"

"Yeah, I know, *don't* call."

"No, I'm here for you, Jake. I don't believe the rumors going around this place. Not for a minute."

"Thanks, Reese." That meant a lot, since Ramsey had been on the team the night Abby died. His injuries from the explosion had left him with a metal plate in his left leg and a painful limp.

Two Feds showed up ten minutes after Jake's call. By then, he was in the gas-station office drinking a soda and watching a rerun on the black and white.

"Reese put an APB out on the woman and the pickup," one of the federal agents informed him. "He suggested you might want to check in with Frank."

Yeah, right. Jake only nodded and took the items he'd requested with a hurried "thanks." He handed them a plastic bag with the handcuffs in it. "You'll find two sets of fresh prints on these. Ask Reese to check them against the files and let me know what he comes up with."

He went into the john and changed quickly into the dry new clothing: jeans, socks, boots, shirt and jean jacket. Then he strapped on the shoulder holster, pocketed the money and slipped the cell phone and extra clips for the weapons into his coat pocket.

As he walked out to the nondescript car waiting for him beside the gas pump, he asked himself: what would Isabella Montenegro do? Probably try to hightail it out of town in the pickup. Just like Reese thought she would. In that case, it would just be a matter of waiting for a call from Reese that she'd been pulled over.

But he no longer believed he was dealing with Isabella Montenegro. He was looking for a woman who'd escaped from a rundown motel in broad daylight, who'd put a shot between a man's eyes without hesitation, who'd pulled a gun on him, handcuffed him to a gas pump, knocked him out and stolen his weapon, money and previously "stolen" truck.

He thought he knew now who he was dealing with. But still, he just couldn't be sure. Not yet. The fingerprints on the handcuffs would tell the tale. But he knew he couldn't wait for that. There was one other way to find out exactly who she was.

He walked to the car and laid his arms over the top. The metal was hot to the touch, the sun low and blinding, the air scented with unleaded gasoline and Texas dust.

That woman, the one who'd known exactly where to point the barrel end of the gun, was too smart not to ditch the truck. But was she smart enough to steal another rig? Did she have the know-how? Abby hadn't been good at appropriating automobiles.

Then what? Another bus? A sound from earlier seemed to echo through his aching head. A train whistle off in the distance.

"Hey," he called back to the gas station attendant. "Is there a passenger train that comes through town?"

The boy nodded, his eyes still glued to the tube. "The Sunset Limited," he called back.

"The one I just heard? Where is it headed?"

"Los Angeles, California." He turned to look at Jake then, as if the words held some sort of magic.

"Do you know what time it left?"

"Eight-thirty. Only time it comes through, headed west."

Jake glanced at his watch. "What's its next stop?"

Chapter Eight

She dozed, waking abruptly to the swaying of the train, and reached automatically for her daughter, fear seizing her for those few seconds before her hand touched warm skin.

Elena slept, curled toward her in the adjacent seat, the morning light on her precious face.

It was impossible now *not* to see Jake in her daughter. For a long time, she just stared down at that face, trying to make sense of everything. Jake was Elena's father. Any fool could see that. But even if she hadn't seen it with her eyes, her heart now knew it was so. Then why didn't her heart tell her that she and Jake had once been lovers?

Her head ached. She felt as if she were trying to put together a puzzle with most of the pieces missing and no idea of the finished picture. Was there any chance at all that Elena *wasn't* her own child?

She thought back to the difficult birth, trying desperately to remember the exact moment she'd first seen her daughter through the flurry of doctors and nurses and the pain. Such pain. The doctor had given her something to help with the birth. He said there was *"una problema."*

She opened her eyes with a start. She *hadn't* seen Elena until after the birth. Long enough after it that she couldn't be sure Elena was the child she'd given birth to.

She felt sick. And weak. And scared. Was it possible? But who would want to do such a thing to her? Calderone had the power, there was no doubt about that. But why would he? Why go to so much trouble? And for what? It made no sense.

She studied Elena, searching for signs of herself in the child, then sighed. It didn't matter if the babies had been switched. Elena was hers. Would always be hers. Calderone be damned. He might have set the wheels in motion, but she was now at the controls.

The thought almost made her laugh. What did she know about control? For the last six years she'd had no control at all over her life.

Just the thought of Julio—had anything he'd told her been true? It didn't appear so. Not based on what she'd seen of herself lately.

She shivered, thinking she should be shocked by her behavior. But she wasn't. She definitely liked this woman better than the defenseless and frightened Isabella Montenegro. But that was the past, she told herself. She wasn't Isabella Montenegro, the woman who took whatever she had to to survive. Not anymore. She was—

She wasn't Abby Diaz, either. Even if she *had* been six years ago, she wasn't that Abby anymore. She didn't know who she was. A stranger. A stranger who was in a lot of trouble, but who was resourceful and strong. It was heady stuff. She liked this new feeling. A lot.

Now all she needed was a plan.

WHEN THE SUNRISE LIMITED stopped in Sanderson, Texas, Jake Cantrell was waiting at the station. He'd driven fast and furiously to beat the train and now kept out of sight, watching to make sure that Isabella and Elena didn't get off. If they were even on the train. His instincts told him that they were. And that wasn't all his instincts told him.

He waited until the last moment before he boarded, getting on the end car. He knew Frank Jordan would be expecting a call. The FBI bureau chief would be furious that he hadn't heard from him.

But Jake didn't work for Frank Jordan anymore. He reported to Mitchell Forbes now and Mitchell gave him free rein. Probably because Mitchell knew him and knew that was the way he worked best. The *only* way he worked now.

Frank should know Jake, too. At least well enough not to be waiting by the phone. They'd once been friends, Frank a mentor, a father figure. They'd worked closely together. Right up until the last case. Right up until the night Abby was killed.

Right or wrong, he blamed the FBI, blamed Frank, for what happened that night. It was supposed to have been part of a routine investigation. They'd been undermanned, not realizing what they'd walked into. One long-time agent, Buster McNorton, had been killed, along with rookies Dell Harper and Abby Diaz. Reese Ramsey had been injured.

Only he and Frank had walked away without injury.

There'd been an investigation, but it hadn't turned up anything at the time. Just bad luck that they'd stumbled onto one of Tomaso Calderone's operations.

Jake had quit the Bureau, bitter as hell because he'd lost everything when he'd lost Abby.

Frank had gone on to work his way up the FBI ladder. So had Reese Ramsey.

He hadn't seen Frank in six years. Hadn't talked to him. And he wasn't ready just yet to call him. Especially after seeing the so-called evidence against him collected by the FBI. Why now, after all these years?

He took a seat by the train window, unable to shake the feeling he'd had since he woke up handcuffed to a gas pump: that he had to get to the woman and kid, pronto. The feeling was so strong, it took everything in him to wait until the train got moving. What if his instincts were wrong? What if she and the kid weren't on the train?

Then that would mean he was wrong about a lot of things.

The train finally pulled out of the station. He watched to make sure she hadn't gotten off. And that Ramon Hernandez hadn't gotten on. At least not while Jake had been sitting at the window. For all he knew, Ramon could have boarded the train at Del Rio.

The thought did nothing to dispel his fears.

He got up and started through the cars.

He hadn't gone far when he spotted the back of the woman's head a few seats ahead and to the right. He'd have recognized that hair and the shape of her head anywhere.

Relief coursed through him. At least he'd been right about her taking the train. Abby had always liked trains. They'd made love the first time on one a lot like this one.

He shook that thought out of his head. He didn't think of her anymore as Isabella Montenegro. But he also hadn't accepted she was Abby. Not yet. He wished he could see the little girl. She had to be with her mother, no doubt sitting in the adjacent seat. As badly as he wanted to make sure, he took a seat a few rows back and off to the left, where he could watch them from behind the magazine he'd bought in the station. He wanted to be ready to move quickly if he had to.

The train rolled along the tracks, with a gentle rocking motion and a faint clickity-clack. With the woman in view, Jake began to relax a little. They appeared to be in no current danger. The car was about two-thirds full and there was no sign of Ramon or any of his men.

Jake leaned back in the seat, willing his heart to

slow, his anxiety to recede. They were fine. His instincts had been right about the train, but wrong about the danger. So where did that leave his other instinct, the one that told him Abby Diaz was alive?

ABBY LOOKED OUT the train window, seeing nothing. She dug in her memory, sifting through the faint and painful nightmares she'd woken with six years before, searching for Abby Diaz, searching for the woman she'd been, frantic to find the skills the FBI agent must have possessed.

She willed herself to remember, needing that training desperately if she hoped to save herself and Elena. But she found nothing in the ashes of her previous life. Except for a few faint recalled feelings.

She had only one memory from before the fire. She cherished it like an old family quilt, wrapping herself in the comforting warmth. Let that one good memory be real, she prayed, as she recalled the feeling that was her grandmother. It filled her with a strange kind of peace. The same kind of peace she'd seen on Elena's face when she looked at her father.

But even the memory of her kind, compassionate, loving grandmother was hard to hold on to. Had she invented the woman just to help her get through the last six years?

What about the only other feeling she could recall? Passion. Had that been with Jake? Was that why she'd blanked out her life prior to six years ago? Because she couldn't face his betrayal?

She felt suddenly bereft. She had no way of knowing who to trust. There was no one to turn to. It was just her and Elena. Just as it had always been. Just as she had always had only one thought: keeping Elena safe. But how?

For a moment, she thought about turning herself over to the FBI. Didn't that make more sense than taking the chance that Calderone's men would capture her and Elena?

She had the sense that she couldn't trust the FBI and absolutely nothing to back up that fear. But the feeling was all she had to go on until she could find out who'd tried to kill her six years ago. And why.

JAKE SAW the woman rise, then the little girl stepped out into the aisle. He felt his heart jump at the sight of the child. She started toward him, her mother right behind her.

He quickly hid behind the magazine, his heart pounding. Any moment they'd walk right by him. Where were they going? Probably just to the bathroom. They were headed in the wrong direction for the dining car. He held his breath as first the child passed by within inches of him, then the woman. She was carrying the bag with the envelope in it.

He wanted to turn and watch them, but waited until he was sure they'd stopped at the bathroom. When he did turn, he saw the waiting line, but no sign of the woman and child. He got to his feet and caught a glimpse of them going into the next car, no doubt hoping to find an empty rest room. He wanted to follow but knew it'd be too risky. Who knew what the woman would do if she spotted him? He couldn't take the chance. Not until the train stopped, anyway.

He sat back down and picked up the magazine again, feeling antsy. Anxious. That feeling he'd had earlier about the woman and child being in imminent danger was back. Only stronger. He glanced around the car. Nothing out of the ordinary. He would bet his horse that Ramon and his men weren't on the train. Then what? What had him so worried?

He turned in his seat to look back. He didn't like letting them out of his sight. But what choice did he have if he hoped to keep his presence a secret? He told himself he could protect them much better at a distance.

When the train stopped in Alpine, he'd get them off. One way or another. At least this time, he knew the woman wouldn't go quietly, as she had in Mexico. He let out a soft laugh. No, he thought, he wasn't dealing with the same woman anymore and they both knew it.

He glanced down at his watch. How long did it take for the two of them to use the bathroom? Even if there had been a line in the next car—

Alarm hurtled through him. It had been too long. They should have been back by now. Something was wrong.

He stood and felt the train begin to slow. They must be nearing the Alpine, Texas station. He moved faster. Out the car and into the next. The car was only about half-full.

He passed the women's bathroom. Vacant. Panic sent a jolt of adrenaline into his system like a strong drug.

There was only one more passenger car. If she wasn't in there— The oppressively hot car was empty. The air-conditioning must have gone out. No wonder it was empty. This bathroom was vacant, as well. He caught a movement outside the railroad car—a flash of bright-colored, billowing fabric and the dark sleeve of a man's suit in the space between the cars. That was when he heard the muffled cry. Then he was running, his weapon drawn.

The train whistle blasted in his ears as he reached the end of the railroad car. In that instant, just before he burst through the door into the enclosed area between the cars, he saw the woman backed against a corner, Elena tucked protectively behind her. A man in a dark suit stood holding a gun on the pair in one gloved hand, his broad back and one shoulder visible through the glass.

Jake hit the door, banging it open, driven by his forward motion and fear. The man in the suit never saw him coming. Never heard him over the blast of the train whistle.

Jake hit the man hard, slamming him into the wall. The gun clattered to the floor. Before the man could reach for it, Abby kicked it away. But the man hadn't been going for the gun, Jake realized belatedly. Instead, he dove for the emergency exit.

Jake grabbed for him, but missed and he was gone, leaping from the slow-moving train into nothing but hot, dry Texas air.

Through the opening, Jake saw him hit the ground and roll, then get to his feet and, limping, disappear behind a parked freight train. Jake gripped the edge of the opening, staring after him, a bad feeling pressing on his chest.

He turned. The woman he no longer thought of as Isabella Montenegro had dropped to her knees and now cradled her daughter in her arms, her eyes tightly closed as she rocked back and forth, murmuring softly. A tear squeezed from beneath her dark lashes to glisten on her cheek.

Just watching her try so hard not to cry—he didn't want to feel this much. He stood for a long moment, letting his heart slow, his fear subside, then he holstered his weapon and reached down with his shirtsleeve over his fingers to pick up the man's gun from the floor. It was a service revolver like the ones used by FBI agents.

The train rolled to a stop, signaling their arrival in Alpine, Texas. The Hub of Big Bend, the sign over the station read, Home of the Last Frontier.

Jake slipped the man's gun into his jacket and picked up the bag she'd dropped, knowing there was little chance of fingerprints since the man had been wearing gloves.

He watched her rise to her feet again, her hands on her daughter's small shoulders as the two turned their gazes to him. Elena smiled at him through her tear-stained face, the look of admiration in her eyes almost his undoing.

"I knew you'd come," she said confidently. "How is your head?"

"OK. Are you all right?"

She nodded and hugged her doll to her, still beaming up at him, her smile contagious. "But Sweet Ana and I still have to go to the bathroom."

He chuckled and shifted his gaze to her mother.

"Thanks," she said.

He wanted to tell her not to thank him. He'd only saved her temporarily and he wasn't sure how long he could keep doing that, because he was no longer sure just who was after her.

But he only nodded and opened the door to the train car, stepping back to let her and Elena enter ahead of him.

Through the window, he could see that the car was still empty. He wondered where Ramon and his men were. But mostly he wondered about the man in the dark suit.

He moved to the door marked ladies' rest room, pulled it open to make sure it really was as vacant as the sign said, then motioned that it was all right for Elena to go on in. "If you don't need your mother's help, she and I will wait here for you."

Her mother's gaze jerked up to his, but she said nothing as Elena closed the door behind her, leaving the two of them alone in the small space between the seats.

"What did that man want with you?" he asked quietly.

She shook her head. "He planned to take us off the train when it stopped. That's all I know."

"You didn't recognize him? He wasn't one of Ramon's men?"

Again she shook her head. "I'd never seen him before." She seemed to hesitate. "But he knew *me*. He was startled when he saw me. It was obvious the way he stared at my face. He called me Abby."

Jake nodded, his heart pounding, as he put down the woman's bag on the floor beside him.

"I'm sorry about earlier." She lowered her gaze. "Back at the gas station."

"Sure you are."

She looked up as if surprised by his reply.

He smiled in answer, searching her face. "We both know that if you had it to do over again, you would."

She said nothing but this time she held his gaze, no longer pretending to be someone she wasn't.

He needed to ask her more about the man who'd been holding them at gunpoint. He needed to ask her a lot of things. But there was one question that couldn't wait. He needed it answered. And he needed it answered now.

Before she knew what was happening, he caught her shoulders and pulled her into him, dropping his lips to hers.

IT HAPPENED too fast. One moment he was simply looking at her. The next he was kissing her. She'd been too stunned. Too shaken from her close call. Too relieved at the sight of him coming to her rescue. Again.

She just hadn't been prepared. But the moment his lips touched hers, she realized nothing could have prepared her for his kiss.

His mouth closed over hers, stealing her breath away. His kiss was at first tentative. Then ravenous. He kissed her deeply, completely, his lips unlocking a memory so pure, so strong, that she felt dizzy and weak under the freedom of it.

His arms enveloped her, pulling her against him, crushing her breasts to his hard muscular chest, kissing her, tasting her, igniting a fuse of desire that quickly spread through her until she thought she'd explode.

It was over far too quickly. He pulled away abruptly, staggering back in the narrow space, his gaze locked on her, his eyes wide.

She leaned against the wall, not trusting her legs as she fought for breath. *This. This* was the feeling she'd told herself she couldn't possibly have remembered.

"Abby," he said.

It was no longer a question. Nor a curse. It was simply a statement of fact.

She was Abby Diaz. And now they both knew it.

Chapter Nine

"Why?" Jake asked in a hoarse whisper. "Why didn't you come back to me?"

She looked into his handsome face, the taste of him still on her lips, the memory of his strong arms around her still making her tremble. His eyes reflected the same hurt and confusion as she felt.

"Abby?" He touched her arm and she shuddered. "Abby, you know me. You know I would never hurt you. Why are you afraid of me?"

"Because I *don't* know you," she cried.

He stared at her, uncomprehending. "You believe that stuff in the envelope about me? Even after that kiss?"

She believed she was Abby Diaz. That she'd been crazy in love with this man. That they shared an incredible passion. But did she really believe he'd tried to kill her six years ago? No. But that was her body talking, and she knew she couldn't trust it right now.

"Are you telling me that kiss meant nothing to you?" he asked, his voice rough with pain.

She shook her head, tears welling in her eyes. "No. Jake, I don't remember anything before waking up in a hospital six years ago."

His jaw dropped. He stared at her openmouthed.

"I woke up to find Julio Montenegro beside my bed. He said he was my husband. All I had of my past was what he told me and some faint memories that made no sense."

Jake shook his head, disbelieving. "You don't still think you're Isabella Montenegro?"

"How can I after everything that's happened? After—" The kiss. She unconsciously ran her tongue over her upper lip, the memory still fresh, the feeling still intoxicating.

"But you're afraid of me because of what you found in the envelope."

She was afraid of him because of the power she knew he had over her, because of the obvious passion they shared. And because she couldn't remember what had happened between them six years ago. But something had. She felt it.

"I don't know who or what to believe at this point," she said, looking away.

From outside, the conductor called "All aboard!"

"If you could remember what you and I had, you'd know the truth," he said softly. "I loved Abby Diaz. I would never have hurt her. We were going to get married. We were going to have a child."

"We *did* have a child," she said.

"Yes." The bathroom door opened and Elena stepped out between them, her doll locked in the crook of her arm.

He seemed to hesitate only a moment before lifting their daughter up into his arms, his face twisted in pain, and hugged her tightly to him. His eyes closed as he buried his face in her hair and breathed in deeply, as if inhaling her essence.

"Daddy," Elena sighed and hugged him around the neck.

Tears burned her eyes, her throat choked closed with emotion, as she watched Jake with his daughter. All those years lost. She felt a surge of anger. Why? Elena had desperately needed a father. Where had Jake been?

"All aboard!" the conductor called again. She could hear the sounds of the train getting ready to move again. Passengers were settling into their seats, voices and laughter drifting down to them.

"We have to get off the train," Jake said and looked up at her as if he expected an argument.

How could she argue? Staying on the train would be foolhardy since someone, whoever he'd been, knew where she was. But was going with Jake any less foolhardy?

She met his gaze, wondering where he planned to take them. What he planned to do with them. Turn them over to the FBI? She looked at her daughter's face. Elena's green eyes glowed as if filled with inner sunshine. After everything that had happened in her young life, all was now right in her world. She'd found her father.

Abby nodded to Jake as her gaze flicked back to him. He wasn't the only one who wanted answers. And while she wasn't ready to trust him with her heart or even her life, she knew she could trust him with Elena's. For now, that was enough. She picked up her bag and started toward the exit.

WITH ELENA still in his arms, he followed Abby through the car, the full weight of responsibility making him tense. Anxious. He didn't know who was after Abby and Elena. Nor what they wanted with the pair. All he knew was that he had to find a safe place to hide them until he could figure it out.

The glaring noonday sun spilled in the windows, blinding and hot. Any moment the train would start moving and they wouldn't be able to get off.

He was right behind her as she scrambled to the platform just seconds before the train started out of the station.

As soon as his feet touched the ground, he was scanning the platform and the cool darkness behind the sun-glazed windows of the station, wary, worried. By now the man who'd jumped from the train could be waiting for them. Or Ramon and his men. Or the Feds. He felt scared. Abby and this child in his arms were everything he'd ever wanted. And now someone was trying to take them away from him—again.

"Here, give me, Elena," Abby said quickly.

The last thing he wanted to do was let go of his daughter. But he was smart enough to know he wouldn't be able to get to his weapon fast enough with the child in his arms. Still, it was all he could do to relinquish her.

The sun hovered overhead. No breeze moved along the tracks. Only the sound of the train leaving the station filled the late morning air.

"On your right," Abby whispered as she took Elena and, smiling, started walking in the other direction.

He glanced out of the corner of his eye and saw the security guards. They were looking at him and talking quickly. One had his hand on the butt end of his gun.

Jake quickly caught up to Abby, slipping his arm around her and leaning closer, as if to share a private thought with her. "Keep moving. They aren't sure yet."

Just before they rounded the corner of the station, Jake called out, "Mom! We almost missed our stop! I hope you haven't been waiting long." Then they were around the blind corner where the guards couldn't see them, couldn't see that no one was waiting to pick them up. "Run!"

ABBY DIDN'T RELAX until Alpine, Texas disappeared behind them, distant as the rugged volcanic-born mountains that cradled it. The day was hot and dry. They were headed south on Farm Road 118 in the four-wheel drive Explorer Jake had rented, leaving behind grassland and commercial orchards for the rough, seemingly endless mountain country ahead, the road behind them almost empty.

"Stealing a car is too risky and it won't buy us any more time than renting one," he'd said a few blocks from the train station after they were sure the security guards hadn't followed. "Not with Calderone *and* the FBI after us now. They'll be on top of anything we do."

She thought of the guards at the train station and wondered who had alerted them. They'd seemed more interested in Jake than her and Elena. Unlike the man on the train. He seemed to know exactly who he was after. The question was why? What had he wanted? By now she wasn't sure who was actually after them. Everyone, it seemed.

She glanced back at Elena, strapped into her seat, her gaze focused on the country outside the window. The child seemed to have gotten over her earlier fear of the sudden change in her mother. Now she watched the rugged terrain flash by, her eyes large, her expression excited. Elena had never been outside the small town in Mexico where she'd been born. Nor had she ever seen mountains before. Elena always made the best of any situation. But this situation continued to get worse.

Abby felt sick to her stomach with fear for her daughter. The people after them were trained killers. They wanted the money Julio had stolen. But did they also want Abby Diaz for some reason? And her child?

Jake turned on the radio and adjusted it so most of the sound came out of the back speakers. "There isn't anywhere we can leave Elena that would be safe," he said quietly as if reading her mind.

She nodded, the lump in her throat making it impossible to speak for a moment. "I'm just worried."

"So am I." He gave her a reassuring smile. "But she should be safe with two former FBI agents taking care of her, don't you think?" His smiled faded in an instant and his eyes darkened to deep jade. "You really don't remember *anything?*" he asked quietly.

She shook her head.

He stared at her for a moment, then the road ahead. "I've heard of cases where there's partial or total memory loss due to a brain injury."

"Mine's not due to an injury."

His gaze ricocheted back to her face. "Then—"

"The doctors said there was nothing physically wrong with me. They think my memory loss was due to shock or repression," she said, watching his face. "Now that I know who I am, I think it was from discovering someone close to me had tried to kill me." She met his gaze and held it.

Jake stared at her for a moment, then looked back to the road ahead. "I didn't try to kill you, Abby. And I'll prove it to you. I'll find out who did."

"*We'll* find out."

He drove in silence for a moment. "You can't remember what happened six years ago?"

"No," she said, hoping she wasn't making a mistake telling him this.

"Or remember…us?"

That was the hardest to admit. "I woke up in a Mexican hospital, burned and in terrible pain, with no memory at all. It's as if my life began six years ago. Julio told me things, but none of the pieces ever fit. I sensed—" A lost passion? "That there was more. Something I'd lost. Something…important."

His gaze softened, and his glance at her was almost a caress. He let out a sigh. "Abby, I can't tell you how much I've missed you. After what happened, I—" He waved a hand through the air. "I didn't want to go on. Not without you."

"But you did." She hadn't meant it to sound like an accusation.

"Yeah, I guess I did." He glanced over at her. "And I guess you still aren't sure about me, are you?"

She wasn't sure about anything. Except that she was Abby Diaz. That Elena was Jake's father. That she and Jake had shared a passion that made her body come alive. Her past played at her memory, bits and pieces that left her worried and afraid of what she'd find when her memory returned. *If* it returned.

"Didn't you ever wonder if I might be alive? Question the idea I was dead?" she asked, hearing the hurt in her words.

"Good Lord, no," he said, reaching over to cup her cheek in his large hand. The hand of a man who worked at hard labor. There was something comforting about that. Strong and solid.

"I saw the end of the building where you'd been just moments before go up in a ball of flame," he said quietly as he turned back to his driving. "I knew you couldn't have survived that."

"But when my body wasn't found—"

"But it was. A body of a woman was found the next day. We just assumed it was yours."

She nodded and hugging herself against the sudden chill, looked away. "I wonder who she was."

"We'll know soon enough," he told her. "Frank is having the body exhumed. But Julio said it was some woman who worked with him."

"How do you explain the evidence I found in the envelope?" she asked, wondering why Julio had planned to burn it. Could he have been trying to protect her? Or someone else?

"I can't," he said simply. "All I can tell you is none of it is true."

They drove along for a few miles to only the sound of Elena singing softly along with the radio.

"Tell me about Abby, the one you knew," she implored. "Tell me what I was like. Who I was. But first, Jake, tell me—was I raised by my grandmother?" She held her breath, terrified of the answer. If that memory hadn't been real, then—

"Ana," he said.

She looked startled.

He nodded. "Yes, the same name you gave Elena's doll."

She frowned. "Julio told me my grandmother was named Carmela. The name sounded wrong. When Elena wanted help naming her doll, I suggested Ana. I liked the name." She looked over at Jake. "The grandmother I remember was a very kind, generous, loving woman."

"She was," he agreed. "You adored her."

Tears filled her eyes. "Is she still alive?"

He shook his head. "Ana Fuentes passed away a year before you were—lost," he finished.

She sighed, relieved to hear that her grandmother hadn't died while she'd been held captive in Mexico. That would have been too painful to bear. "And my parents?"

He shook his head again. "Your father died before you were born. Your mother when you were just a baby."

How odd to lose both parents at such a young age. "From accidents?"

Jake nodded, but kept his eyes on the road. Was there more to it?

She stared out at the rugged scenery. "Then I had no one."

"Just me," Jake said.

She realized they were nearing some sort of town. She could see a handful of adobe and rock dwellings, but they seemed deserted.

"Study Butte?" Elena said, leaning over the front seat, to read the sign.

"Stew-dy Butte," he corrected.

As they drew closer, Abby saw that the town was

abandoned, the buildings mostly in ruin. "A ghost town," she whispered and looked over at Jake, wondering why he'd brought them here, of all places.

He didn't say anything as he drove through the deserted town, then took a narrow dirt road that led up into the hills.

He glanced over at her. "Remember any of this?"

She shook her head. Nothing in the harsh landscape looked familiar. Just isolated and hostile.

"This is where I was raised," he said after they'd driven up the windy road for a few minutes. "Study Butte was a mining town. My grandfather got in on the last of the quicksilver just before it died out." He glanced over at her. "Like you, I was raised by a grandparent."

She heard something in his voice she recognized. Regret. Pain. Loss. "What happened to your parents?"

"They weren't into parenting," he said tightly. He brought the car to a stop in front of a small adobe building. "My grandfather came to the house one night and brought me here."

She swallowed, her eyes burning, and reached across to squeeze his hand on the seat between them.

"It wasn't that bad," he said, and withdrew his hand, pushing away her sympathy. "I learned to love it here. My grandfather was a lot like your grandmother. He saved me."

"So we were both orphans," she said.

"Yeah." He glanced over the seat at Elena, the lines in his face softening. "Come on," he said to the child as he shut off the engine. "There's something I want to show you."

Elena scrambled from the car to be hoisted up into his strong arms. He looked over at Abby as she got out of the car and tilted his head toward the steep hillside behind the house. The trail up the mountain was faint from lack of use. She glanced back the way they'd come, at the ghost town, now miniature in the distance. Then she followed Jake and Elena up the path through the rocks and cactus.

She could hear Jake pointing out mountains and flowers to Elena.

"What is that smell?" Elena asked, wrinkling up her nose.

He laughed. "Creosote bush," he said pointing to the short evergreen with tiny yellow flowers on it. "That is the smell of the desert."

They topped the ridge, stopping in the hollow of a rock outcropping. Jake moved to the edge where the rocks opened. She joined him and caught her breath at the sight before her. The landscape was honeycombed with canyons and caves against a backdrop of jagged mountains, some reddish with the cinnabar that had contained the mercury, the substance that had given the town life—and killed it. Beyond Study Butte, she could see the river that marked the boundary between Texas and Mexico.

"The Rio Grande," he said proudly as if it was his.

In some way, she realized it was. This was Jake's home. That place he could always come to that resonated with another time. Did she have such a place?

"The Rio Grande is one of the longest rivers in North America," he was telling Elena.

She felt his gaze on her.

"You should see the sunsets up here," he said quietly.

She met his eyes and felt a heat hotter than even the fiery sun hanging in the endless blue overhead. And she knew they'd seen a few sunsets up here, that they'd made love in the hollow of these rocks.

He seemed lost in her eyes as if he could see things she couldn't, feel things she could only imagine.

"I'm hungry," Elena said. "Is this where we're going to eat the food we bought?"

He dragged his gaze away and laughed. "This is the place."

He started back down the mountainside, but Abby stayed behind for a few moments, trying to see Jake Cantrell as a boy here, wanting to feel the strong roots that had helped form the man.

Something caught her eye. She leaned closer and saw the small hollow in the rocks where the sun glistened off one side. Initials had been laboriously dug into the stone. J.C.

JAKE TOOK the trail down to the house, surveying the dirt road and the familiar hills around it. Elena was at his side. He knew he hadn't been followed from Alpine. Traffic had been light, and once he'd turned at Study Butte, he'd had the road to himself.

Nor did anyone know about this place. Not even Mitchell. Or the FBI. The only person he'd ever shared it with was Abby. And now his daughter.

As he pointed out the different mountains in the distance to Elena, he felt himself beginning to relax. He hadn't been back here in years. But he *had* kept the place after his grandfather died. A couple from town took care of the upkeep and he kept his name off the title, burying it under a variety of company names and addresses.

He hadn't done it out of paranoia, but the simple desire for privacy. Study Butte was too much of himself. He hadn't wanted to share that part of him with anyone. Except Abby.

He turned to look back at her. Her dark hair shone in the sunlight. It swung around her shoulders as she moved toward him, her hips swaying, thighs strong and muscular against the denim of her jeans, the soft hint of her breasts beneath the embroidered top.

"Did you see the mountains?" Elena asked excitedly. "Daddy says they named a canyon in Big Bend just for me. Santa Elena Canyon. He says the walls of the canyon are so high and narrow that the river roars through it. The Apaches used to believe that anyone who went into the canyon would never be seen again."

Abby laughed, the sound heartrending.

Jake wished there was a place that the three of them could go and never be seen again.

"Can we go there someday? Can we see it?" Elena pleaded.

Abby ran a hand over her daughter's dark hair and smiled. "Yes," she said after a moment. "I suppose we could someday." She looked up at him for confirmation.

"Definitely. The three of us."

Elena squealed in delight and ran to the car to help with the groceries.

He could see the doubt on Abby's face. "No one knows about this place but you and me. It's going to be all right."

She nodded.

"Or is it me who has you worried?"

She seemed to study him for a moment, then shook her head.

He stepped closer to her, his fingers caressing her smooth cheek as he brushed back her dark hair. Her body came to him as if drawn by magnetism. Or something much more powerful.

He turned her, spooning her body to his as he wrapped her in his arms so they were both facing east. "That's Big Bend," he whispered. "And someday we'll take our daughter there to see her canyon."

Abby leaned back against him. Her scent mingled with the desert's. He closed his eyes, breathing it in, letting himself believe for that moment that she was finally starting to trust him and that they were safe.

THE ADOBE DWELLING was small but cozy—and almost familiar, Abby thought, with its tiled floors and wood and wicker furniture.

Jake motioned to the huge claw-foot tub in the bathroom. "If you ladies would like to get a hot bath, I'll get dinner started."

A bath. At that moment, Abby couldn't imagine anything she wanted more.

"Can we have bubbles?" Elena asked excitedly.

Jake produced a bottle of purple bubble bath from the bag of groceries. "Just for you," he said handing it to Elena. "I *thought* a girl like you would appreciate a bubble bath."

Elena giggled as she took the plastic bottle and ran into the bathroom. Jake handed Abby the other supplies he'd bought while she was purchasing clothing for her and Elena. Their fingers brushed and she felt a rush both chemical and electrical. Her breath caught in her throat as a memory flashed bright as Texas sunlight.

"What is it?" Jake asked, suddenly wary.

She stared at him. "I…I think it's a memory. You and me on a…train? Just the two of us."

He smiled, relief softening his strong, masculine face. "What do you remember?" he asked gently, seductively.

She felt her face flush with heat, the images so provocative, so sensual, so…sexy. She swallowed. "Just that we were on a train together before today."

He nodded, studying her as if he didn't quite believe that was all she'd seen.

"Mommy! Come on!" Elena called from the bathroom.

Face burning, she hurried in to join her daughter, closing the bathroom door behind her. In the mirror over the sink, she saw her high color and knew he'd seen it as well. The images of their lovemaking had burned into her brain like a brand. Her skin tingled with the memory, her breasts heavy and aching, need making her weak. How odd to remember such intimacies with a man who was still a stranger to her! Worse yet, to want him so desperately.

She filled the tub, bathing Elena first, then shooing her daughter out to help Jake with dinner so she could be alone. She poured in the purple bubble bath. It smelled of lilac. She stepped into the warm water and cool lilac bubbles and slid down with a satisfied *"Ahhhhhh."*

Closing her eyes, she reclined in the tub, bubbles up to her chin, and tried not to think about the man in the next room. Impossible! She opened her eyes, remembering the two of them on that other train, remembering enough to make her ache with unbearable longing.

Over dinner, Jake talked about his childhood while they ate fried catfish, hush puppies and coleslaw. Then he told Elena about her great-grandmother Ana. Abby listened, her eyes tearing. She wished Ana could have lived to see Elena, but more than anything, she wished Elena could have known her great-grandmother.

Elena listened, eyes wide, to Jake's stories, giggling one minute, bashful the next when he turned the full power of his smile on her. Abby's heart ached watching the two of them.

After dinner, Jake carried a tuckered-out Elena up to one of the two bedrooms. Abby stood in the doorway, listening to the two of them talking quietly, their voices blending in a sweet lullaby.

She watched him lean down to kiss the child on the cheek. Elena grasped him around the neck with both of her small arms and pulled him close.

"Good night, Daddy." She kissed his cheek.

Jake straightened. Abby could see the effect the words had on him. The effect his daughter had on him. He cleared his throat. "Good night, *chica suena.*"

Elena giggled. "That's what Mommy calls me."

"I know. It's what her grandmother called her."

"Good night, Mommy," she called out as she circled an arm around Sweet Ana, snuggled down under the comforter he pulled over her, and smiled up at him.

Abby had to turn away. She walked out onto the portico and stared up at the magnificent sky. Earlier, the purple tint of twilight had softened the rough edges of the mountains. Now they were etched black against the vast Texas horizon. Stars shimmered in the deep dark blue overhead, dusting the quiet evening in silver starlight. The breeze was warm and dry, perfumed with a mixture of desert scents that pulled at her memory.

She hugged herself and looked up at the heavens,

asking the one question that had haunted her since she'd learned of Jake Cantrell's existence.

"Wishing on a star?" he asked from behind her.

Startled, she swung around. His broad shoulders filled the doorway, blocking out the faint glow of the light he'd left on inside. Slowly he stepped into the starlight.

"Abby." His fingertips found her face, warm and gentle.

She lost herself in his look, in his touch, stepping into his powerful embrace as if opening a familiar door.

His kiss was both soft and seductive, passionate and potent. He traced her lips with the tip of his tongue. She opened to him, breathless, heart pounding, body aching.

"Jake," she whispered against his lips. A plea.

He pulled back just enough to look down into her face. Then he swept her up in his arms and, opening the screen door with the toe of his boot, carried her into the bedroom and laid her carefully on the bed.

"It's been a long time," she whispered as he joined her. Starlight filtered in through the curtains along with the sweet warm scent of the night breeze.

His gaze touched her face gently. "How long?"

"Six years."

He frowned. "You don't mean—"

"Julio was never a husband to me."

He drew her to him. "I wish I could say I was sorry," he said huskily. Then his lips dropped to hers and he took her mouth with a hunger that could only match her own.

Frantically they made love, stripping away clothing to get to bare skin, kissing and caressing, wrapped up, locked together, unwilling to relinquish even a naked inch of the other's body until the moment when they lay spent, hearts pounding in unison.

Abby sighed and looked up into his handsome face. "Jake." Her one question had been answered. She remembered him…them. Their shared passion. This had been the one feeling she'd recalled, the feeling she hadn't trusted. She'd been afraid to trust it, for fear it had never existed.

They made love again, this time, slowly, seductively. She explored his body, he explored hers. The night waned outside the window, they reveled in rediscovering what they'd thought they'd lost forever.

How could she question any longer who she was? Or that Jake had been the man she'd shared such passion with? How could she still wonder if he'd been the one who'd tried to kill her?

She lay curled in his arms, sated and satisfied, feeling blessed. Feeling lucky. Both feelings scared her. She'd learned with Julio never to feel safe. Never to let her guard down. With Jake, could she and Elena learn to feel safe again?

She left the warmth of his arms to check on Elena. The child slept, Sweet Ana beside her. Abby covered her with the thin blanket and padded back across the hall to Jake.

He must have seen the worried look on her face.

"You and I are the only ones who ever knew about this place," he said. "If we aren't safe here, Abby, we aren't safe anywhere."

She nodded, fearing the latter was true as she got back into the bed, back into his arms. But she couldn't shake the worried feeling that this wouldn't last. Couldn't last.

"Tell me about the last six years," he whispered against her hair. "Please."

She stared up at the fan turning hypnotically above them, the air cool on her naked skin. "Elena and I were virtually prisoners. I tried to leave once." She hesitated. "Julio caught me and Elena. I knew then that he'd kill us both if I tried again. I also knew he was involved with Calderone. I hoped pretending would keep Elena safe."

He didn't say anything for a long time, just held her. "I'm sorry. Why do you think he pretended to be your husband for all those years?"

She shook her head. "I guess he planned to use me and Elena to get him out of Mexico with Calderone's money." Why did she feel it was much more than that? "I suppose once he realized I had amnesia and was pregnant, it was an easy way to keep an eye on me. Plus he had his own built-in housekeeper and cook."

She saw Jake's jaw clenched with anger and changed the subject.

"Tell me about my life. The key has to be in my past and you're the only one who can help me."

He told her about a strong, capable, sexy, interesting, unique woman named Abby Diaz and she had to laugh, knowing that no such woman had ever existed, except in Jake's mind. Or maybe his heart.

She tried to imagine even a scaled-down version of that woman, that life, but still couldn't.

"Has any of your memory come back?" he asked.

"Just feelings more than actual memories. Images." She frowned. "I keep seeing an older, blond woman, a striking woman."

"Crystal Jordan. Frank's wife. We spent quite a lot of time at their place. The four of us and some of the other agents."

She frowned, trying to pull up something that seemed just on the edge of her memory. But gave up after a moment and closed her eyes, her head aching.

"Give it time, Abby."

"I might not have time," she whispered. "Jake, there is someone in my past who I can't trust, who might still want me dead—and I won't even recognize him when he comes for me."

"What about the man on the train? You still can't place him?"

She shook her head. "I just know that he was shocked to see me. He definitely recognized me, and it surprised him."

He told her about the six-agent team that had gone into the building the night she disappeared, then described the agents.

"Buster McNorton was older, a veteran, experienced and levelheaded," he said summing it up.

"He's one of those who died?"

Jake nodded. "The other agent who died was Dell Harper."

She felt a small stir of memory. "Dell?"

Jake seemed to be watching her closely. "Dell Harper was the quiet type. Average Joe. You were closer to him than anyone else on the team."

That surprised her. "Really?"

He looked away. "You were on his baseball team. You always said he was like the little brother you never had."

She studied Jake, sensing something she couldn't put her finger on as she tried to picture Average Joe Dell Harper. "Was Dell married?"

He shook his head. "I think I heard something about a fiancée once. But I guess she was killed in an accident." He seemed to hesitate. "You were always real protective of him. He might have told you about it."

She said nothing, wondering if she'd heard something in Jake's voice. Jealousy?

"Frank and Reese Ramsey stayed with the Bureau," Jake continued. "Both have moved up. You remember Reese?"

She shook her head. She didn't remember any of

this. It seemed as foreign as the stories Julio had told her. She wondered if she and Jake would have still been with the Bureau if that night hadn't gone so badly.

"Reese is a nice guy. Smart, easygoing, dedicated, but not like Frank."

"You don't like Frank?" she asked, surprised considering that he'd just told her they'd spent a lot of time with Frank and his wife, Crystal.

"I used to, but everything changed when you—"

"Were lost," she suggested, using his words.

"Yeah."

"Frank was with us that night?" she asked.

He let out a sigh. "Frank had gone around to the side of the building with Reese. You and I were taking the front." He looked up, his gaze meeting hers for an instant. "I'm not sure what happened. One minute you were behind me. The next you'd gone around to the back after Buster and Dell."

A chill raced over her skin like a long-legged spider. She shivered. Why had she gone with Buster and Dell instead of staying with Jake? She wouldn't have disobeyed orders, would she? She snuggled into him, suddenly terrified.

"You think Frank ordered me to go with Buster and Dell?"

He said nothing, just pulled her close and kissed the top of her head.

"If that's true, then what are we going to do? That would mean that Frank—"

His cell phone rang, startling them both. He looked at her for a long moment, then he reached for the phone where he'd left it beside the bed. He acted as if he knew who was calling. A man they both suspected they now had to fear.

Chapter Ten

But it wasn't Frank Jordan's voice on the other end of the line. "Jake?"

"Reese." He sat up, glancing over at the clock beside the bed. Two-fifteen in the morning. What was Reese doing calling at this hour?

"Do you have Isabella Montenegro and her daughter with you?" Reese said without preamble, his tone hurried.

"Yes, what—"

"Jake, you're in danger."

He almost laughed. He'd been in danger since the moment he took this assignment.

"You need to get the woman and child to us as soon as possible," Reese was saying. "Tell me where you are and I'll send—"

"Reese, what's going on?"

"Jake, you've been set up. The woman isn't Abby Diaz. Your life is in danger as long as—"

"What the hell are you talking about?" he demanded.

"The fingerprints you sent us from the hand-cuffs," Reese said. "They *aren't* Abby Diaz's."

He felt the blood rush from his head, the earth drop beneath him as if he were suddenly marooned in outer space. He glanced over at her, lying beside him on the bed. She looked up at him, fear in her eyes.

"What is it?" she whispered.

"That's not possible," he said into the phone.

"Abby's dead, Jake. We exhumed the body. It's her. There's no doubt. You've got to bring the woman in. And the kid. And you have to hurry."

He fought for breath, his mind screaming, *no!*

"Jake, it's a trap. Don't be a damned fool. Wher-ever you are, get the hell out of there. Now. Before it's too late. I'll send men to meet you. Just tell me where—"

He closed his eyes. "I'll take care of it myself," he said and clicked off the phone, dropping it to the floor.

"Jake," she whispered beside him. "What is it?"

He didn't look at her. He couldn't. He got up and pulled on his jeans. "It was Reese Ramsey. I sent him the handcuffs you used to cuff me at the station. He checked the prints." He turned then to face her. "He says they aren't Abby Diaz's prints."

She stared up at him, looking stunned, confused, then dropped her gaze to the crumpled bedsheets.

"The body they exhumed from the grave," he continued. "It's been positively identified by the FBI as Abby Diaz's."

She shook her head, her eyes filling with tears as her gaze rose again to his. "The person who called, he's the one you said you trusted?"

Jake nodded, sick at heart. And scared. He tugged on his shirt, his flesh still alive with the feel of her, his body already aching for her.

"Of course, it's a lie," he said quietly. "Someone falsified the report. There's no other explanation."

She nodded, her eyes on him. "Frank?"

"He'd have the authority." He stood, fighting the need to flee, fighting the question that haunted him. If he didn't believe what Reese had told him about Abby, then why did he believe the part about the trap, about being in immediate danger?

"I think we'd better get out of here," he said, feeling the weight of his words, the implications weighing on him.

"I'll get Elena." She rose and dressed quickly, no longer looking at him.

He watched her leave the room, his heart hurting, the pounding too loud. Reese had to be wrong. About everything. He hadn't even realized how hard he'd been listening until he heard the sound outside. A sound as distinct as a heartbeat and as ominous as a gunshot. Someone tried the back door.

If we aren't safe here, we're not safe anywhere. His words had come back to haunt him.

MOONLIGHT MADE a silver path on the tile floor as she padded quickly across the hall to Elena's room.

She felt numb. All except her heart, which seemed to struggle with each labored beat. *Not Abby Diaz.*

Jake's words had stunned her. Not Abby Diaz? Just when she'd finally found herself? Just when she'd found Jake and the passion she'd remembered from before?

It was one thing to want to take away her new-found strength, to take away her identity, to take Jake and the love she'd once shared, but to take her child, to make her believe the babies *had* been switched and that Elena wasn't hers—because Elena was so obviously Jake Cantrell's daughter.

She looked down at her daughter. Elena lay curled in the narrow bed, burrowed deep in the blankets, only the top of her dark head showing. Anger made her weak. Who was playing with her life like a puppeteer, pulling her heartstrings? If only she could remember the past. The answer had to be there. The person behind this. The person responsible for trying to destroy her.

But what made her heart ache was what she'd witnessed in Jake's eyes. She'd seen that moment of doubt. That moment of distrust.

As she reached down to pick up her daughter, a shadow moved across the window on the other side of the curtain. She froze as the outline of one man, then another, crept along the side of the house. Hurriedly she scooped Elena up, covers and all.

Elena's eyes widened as she came awake.

"Shhh," she whispered to the child. "Not a sound."

She started out of the room, desperate to get back to the bedroom and Jake. But as she reached the hall, Elena in her arms, Elena cried out. "Sweet Ana! I dropped Sweet Ana!"

Then the air exploded with the crash of shattering glass and splintering wood as the house was breached.

She looked up to see Jake framed in the bedroom doorway across the hall, a gun in his hand. She heard him call a warning. Out of the corner of her eye, she caught movement. Shielding Elena, she ran toward him.

Jake got off one shot before he took the bullet. She felt it whiz past her, saw it strike him, his head jerking back, and watched in horror as he went down.

She lurched toward him but was grabbed from behind before she could reach his side or the weapon he'd dropped to the floor next to him. Elena was pulled from her arms and she was dragged backward. The last thing she saw was one of Ramon's men kneel beside Jake and shake his head.

She started to scream. But a hand closed over her mouth and nose, the cloth wet and cold, the smell strong and blinding. Her knees gave way beneath her. And she fell, dropping into blackness as if falling down a deep, dark bottomless well.

ABBY WOKE to the dark and the silence and the pain. So much like six years ago when she'd awakened in the Mexican hospital. Only this time, she knew what she'd lost. This time, she remembered too much.

"Elena?" she whispered as she sat up and felt around on the cold floor for her daughter. "Elena?"

She felt nothing but the rough adobe of her prison. Panic seized her as she stumbled to her feet, windmilling her arms in the blinding blackness. "Elena!"

Her knuckles scraped the wall. Pain shot up her arm, but her real pain centered in her pounding heart. She took slow, deep breaths, but they came out as sobs. Where was Elena? Her baby? What had they done with her?

Elena was gone. Jake was dead. Shot dead. Jake. Oh, God. Jake. Had he died believing her an imposter? Part of a plot to get him killed?

She closed her eyes against the thought. Someone with the FBI had falsified the fingerprint and autopsy reports. It had to have come from the top. Frank. But why?

She fought the urge to scream. But screaming wouldn't bring Jake back. Hysteria wouldn't help Elena. She had to think of her daughter now. She dropped to her hands and knees, her legs too weak to hold her, her head hurting too much to think of anything but her child.

She felt her way around the room. It was small, no more than a cell, and completely empty. The walls were adobe like the floor, rough and cold to the touch. On one wall, she found a door, thick and made of wood. She put her shoulder to it. It didn't budge.

She sat back down on the floor, dizzy from the darkness and the chloroform or whatever they'd used to knock her out. She felt cold and nauseous, sick soul-deep. Jake was dead. Elena lost. Defeated, she wrapped her arms around her knees, laid her head down and cried.

The sound of the bolt scraping in the lock on the other side of the door made her lift her head. Hurriedly, she dried her eyes, wishing she had something to use as a weapon. The door slowly swung open, bringing with it the night breeze. And light. She blinked. A man stood silhouetted in the doorway, holding an old-fashioned lantern. He shone the light into the room, blinding her. She heard his sharp intake of air.

"Get her out of there," he ordered in Spanish.

His voice was at once familiar—and frightening, because she couldn't place it. She got to her feet, pulling herself up the rough wall, shielding her eyes from the light. Two men came into the room and, taking her arms, dragged her out into a hallway of sorts. Some of the walls had eroded away, leaving dark holes open to the night.

She only half feigned the weakness that made it hard for her to stand. They held her up in the light of the lantern. Slowly, she lifted her head.

He stood only inches away, studying her. When she dared look up into his face, she was afraid she'd know him and afraid she wouldn't.

He was tall, with brown hair and a kind face. But his angry expression and the intense look in his dark eyes made her recoil inwardly. She told herself she'd never seen him before. But the look in those eyes assured her it was not mutual.

"My God," he said in English. "Abby?"

"Where is my daughter?"

He seemed taken back by her tone. "Don't worry about her. She's fine. Being well cared-for." He shook his head, his gaze studying her face with astonishment. "Jake must have been shocked when he saw you."

Something in his words... A memory dropped into place. A flash of knowledge she didn't question. As sure as the shots she'd fired from the pistol. "Isn't that the way you planned it, Frank?"

JAKE WOKE to an unbearable sense of loss that blunted his physical pain.

Death, he realized, came in many forms. He felt the crease where the bullet had grazed his head. He was weak from loss of blood. It took all of his strength to crawl into a sitting position. He leaned back against the wall. Blood ran down into his left eye. Images moved across his memory, dark and debilitating. Abby. He swallowed and tasted blood. A trap.

His, it seemed, was a death of despair.

Slowly, he shrugged out of his shirt and, balling it up, pressed it to the shallow ditch-like wound that started at his forehead, ending just over his left ear.

The breeze flapped at the curtains of the broken window. The front door stood open at an odd angle. It had been a trap, all right. And he'd walked right into it.

He felt too weak to move, too heartsick to know what to do if he did. He knew now that he'd been fighting an uphill battle against a power much stronger and more far-reaching than himself. Even if he knew who'd taken Abby and Elena, even if he could find them, he wasn't sure he could save them. He wasn't even sure he could save himself at this point.

Then in the shaft of moonlight that spilled across the tile floor, he saw something. His heart constricted. He rolled over onto his right elbow and scooted along the floor, still holding the shirt to his head, still unable to stand, barely able to see.

When he was close enough, he sat back against the wall again, sucked in hard breaths, and slowly pulled the object he'd spotted to him. Sweet Ana. He pressed the worn rag doll to his face. It smelled of lilac bubble bath. It smelled of Elena.

Emotion choked off his throat. He closed his eyes and tipped his head back, wanting to howl like the coyotes in the night. He'd lost so much. He couldn't lose any more. He crushed the doll in his hands, the way he wanted to crush the people who'd done this.

With all sensation centered on the pain in his head and heart, at first he didn't feel the tiny, cold, stabbing pain in the palm of his right hand. Slowly he opened his eyes and focused on the doll and his large sun-browned hands gripping it.

He opened his fists. The soft fabric was forgiving. He brushed his fingers over the handmade dress. It matched the one Elena had worn just yesterday. He stared down into Sweet Ana's face, for the first time noticing her stitched eyes. Cantrell green. And with a cold chill, he realized how Julio had planned to get out of Mexico with the money—and his life.

He tossed aside his bloody shirt and struggled to his feet, moving as quickly as he could before blood blurred his vision again. Stumbling into the kitchen, he set the doll down on the counter and dug in the drawer for a sharp knife. Lifting the hem of the doll's dress to expose the stitching along the right side of the stuffed body, he carefully cut through the threads until he saw the sharp edge of the key hidden inside.

Chapter Eleven

"You know who I am?" Frank Jordan sounded surprised.

"Just like you know who *I* am."

He raised a brow, the light from the lantern flickering in the warm night breeze. He looked older than she remembered him. His hair grayer. His eyes more anxious.

"Not Abby Diaz. She's dead." His words sent a chill through her.

"I guess you'd probably know that better than anyone."

He frowned and motioned for the men to release her and leave.

She straightened, willing herself to stand taller in front of him, to show no fear. An impossible task, knowing now the influence a man in his position could wield.

She recognized the guards as two of Calderone's men as they left, disappearing down the long, dark hallway toward a faint light, leaving her alone with Frank.

She looked at him and swallowed, her throat dry, her eyes burning with tears at the memory of Jake lying on the floor and with anger at seeing Frank Jordan here with Calderone's men. If she'd had a weapon she'd have used it on Jordan without a second thought. If she could have taken him with her bare hands, she'd have tried.

"I want to see my daughter," she repeated.

"She has Jake's eyes," he mused. "And your beauty." His gaze seemed to focus on her and soften. "And you have Abby's face and her temper."

"That's odd, since the FBI is trying to convince me I'm an imposter."

Frank's gaze narrowed. "Too bad you didn't listen."

Another memory came out of nowhere just like the last one had. *Frank calling her into his office the morning of the explosion. Acting upset with her and threatening to suspend her from duty.* The realization made her heart pound. But why? She couldn't remember why.

"Let's go out here where we can talk in private," he said and motioned to an opening in the wall that led to an old courtyard. In the lantern's glow, she could see the courtyard had fallen into ruin, just as it appeared the rest of the building had over the years.

He indicated a rock bench near a crumbling foun-

tain and she gladly sat down, still weak from the
drug they'd used on her and a little disoriented. She
realized the building reminded her of the ones they'd
driven by in Study Butte. She sniffed the breeze and
smelled creosote. Was it possible they were still in
the ghost town?

He put the lantern down on the edge of the foun-
tain and sat down next to it. No one would have
ever guessed he was FBI, dressed as he was now in
a T-shirt, lightweight jacket, jeans and hiking boots.
Except for the bulge of his service revolver under
his jacket.

"Your men killed Jake," she said, her voice no
more than a whisper. She remembered enough about
Frank to know he wouldn't have done it himself.
And surprisingly found it a flaw in his character. But
she knew from the way Calderone's men were taking orders from him that he was responsible.

"If Jake had done as he was supposed to…" His
voice broke. "He was never good at following orders."

"Who do you take your orders from, Frank?" she
asked. "Tomaso Calderone?"

He raised his gaze to meet hers, his jaw tightening, but said nothing as he studied her, as if he really
wasn't sure who she was. Or maybe, he was just
worried about how much she'd remembered.

"Why did you try to suspend me that day? Because you knew the team was walking into a trap?"

He seemed surprised that she'd remembered their

last meeting. His face flushed. "I thought you had amnesia. Julio said—"

"I thought you said Abby Diaz was dead." The anger bubbled up, hot as liquid lava. "You *knew* I was alive in Mexico. Maybe you were even the one who ordered me captured and held prisoner all those years."

He flinched at the words. "Do you really think I'd have left you there if I'd known?"

"You're doing your best to make people think I'm dead," she snapped. "I wouldn't put anything past you."

He met her gaze in the lantern light, his eyes hard. "You were always so smart, one hell of an FBI agent. Too bad you've forgotten your training."

She stared at him. "Don't worry, it's coming back. I know Julio was working for you." Was Frank the man Elena said Julio used to call in the States? "Are you going to stand there and tell me you didn't know I was his prisoner for the last six years?"

"I only found out you might be alive a few days ago when Julio Montenegro told me," he said evenly. "I didn't believe him."

"Then why did you send Jake? Why not come yourself?"

He got to his feet and moved away, never completely turning his back on her. The man was no fool. She listened for Elena and sounds beyond the thick adobe walls, but heard nothing that would indicate where Elena was being held or if her daughter was even here. She watched Frank and waited for an opportunity.

"Why did I send Jake?" He turned to meet her gaze. "Because I couldn't face doing it myself."

She saw something in his eyes. A weakness that ran bone-deep. And guilt. "You were in charge of that routine investigation that night. How did it turn out to be one of Calderone's warehouses? You had to have set us up. But why? Why would you get involved with Calderone? Didn't you have enough power, enough money, enough influence over enough lives? Or is there just no limit for you?"

His eyes darkened in the lantern light as if her words cut him to the quick. "You're wrong, Abby."

It was the first time he'd called her by name and something in his tone stilled her. She watched him glance up at the sky that had just begun to lighten over the tile roof top.

"We don't have much time," he said quietly. "You need to tell me where Julio hid the money. It's the only hope you and your daughter have of staying alive."

"YOU NEED a doctor," the elderly Mexican woman said as she pressed the wet cloth to Jake's head and turned a worried eye on what the attackers had done to his house.

He held on to the chair waiting for the dizziness and darkness to subside. "No doctor." He'd called the Mexican couple who took care of his house because he knew if anyone could patch him up and get him on his feet it would be Guadalupe.

She shook her head, her lips pursed in disapproval. "You are lucky you are not dead."

"I thought I *was*." He closed his eyes as she applied the alcohol, gritting his teeth.

"There is much blood, but the bullet only grazed your hard head," she said. "You have the lives of a cat."

He'd gotten himself to the bathroom mirror and had almost passed out at the sight of the blood and the wound. That's when he'd called her. She was right. He was damned lucky to be alive. But it meant nothing without Abby and Elena.

While Guadalupe bandaged his head and gave him three extra-strength pain relievers, her husband boarded up the windows and door of the house. When she'd finished, he thanked her.

"If you bleed to death, you don't thank me," she said.

He smiled at her. "You and Alejandro are good friends." He walked her to the door. Alejandro had finished his temporary repairs to the house and now stood looking back down the road toward Study Butte.

"What is it?" Jake asked, joining the elderly man.

"Lights," he said. "In the old mining building."

Jake looked to where he pointed. "You're sure no one is living there? Squatters?"

Alejandro shook his head. "It is uninhabitable."

"Take the back way home to Teringua," he told his friend. "Be careful."

"Vaya con Dios," Guadalupe said as they left. Go with God.

Jake went back inside and picked up the key he'd found in the doll from the table. Stamped on the metal were the words El Paso Central, locker No. 19. He pocketed it and tucked Sweet Ana into Abby's bag along with the rest of their clothing, the cell phone and the manila envelope about Abby, then zipped the bag shut.

How had someone known about Study Butte? Known he would come here? No one could have.

"I'M NOT TELLING you anything until I see my daughter," Abby said, assuring herself Frank Jordan didn't have the stomach for torture.

He rubbed his hand over his face, then studied her as if she were a problem he didn't have an answer for. "Fine. But you're wasting valuable time."

"Does Elena know—"

"About Jake?" He shook his head.

She nodded, thankful for that, and rose to her feet to be led through the abandoned adobe building. It didn't appear to be a house; it was too large for that and arranged all wrong.

At one point she caught sight of a mountainside through a hole in the wall. They *were* still in Study Butte! She felt her heart soar with hope. If she could reach Elena and get away, she could find a place for them to hide. But those were some pretty big ifs.

Elena was sitting on a wooden stool at an old desk, picking at a peanut-butter-and-jelly sandwich when Abby came into the room. She recognized the large Mexican man who stood over the child and the two others sitting in the glass-less windowsill appearing to watch the road below. All three were armed. All three were Calderone's men.

Elena's face lit up when she saw her. She jumped down from the wooden stool to run into her mother's arms.

"Mommy," she cried and hugged her tightly. "Sweet Ana is lost and I'm scared and you know I don't like peanut butter."

She smiled down at her daughter. "Don't worry about Ana. We'll find her." She eyed the large man still standing guard near the table and could feel Frank's presence behind her. She ignored the others. "She doesn't like peanut butter. Do you have anything else she could eat?"

The large man looked put upon. "What kind of kid doesn't like peanut butter?"

"A kid raised on tortillas and goat cheese," Ramon said, and laughed as he got up and walked toward Abby.

She recognized his voice. He greeted her in Spanish as if they were old friends. In fact, now that she could put his voice with his face, she realized she had seen him at the villa with Julio on more than one occasion.

"Did she tell you where the money is?" Ramon asked Frank.

"Not in front of the child," Frank said under his breath. "Carlos, get the girl something decent to eat from the store. Bring us all something."

The large man seemed to hesitate, his gaze going to Ramon for approval. "The store won't even be open this time of the morning."

"Then break in," Frank snapped.

Ramon moved, just inches from Frank's face. His voice dropped, a warning in his look, in his words. "I don't like being here. We should have taken the woman and kid and gotten away from here. But I agreed to do it your way. Now I want to know what the holdup is. Let's get what we need from the woman and get out of here. If you can't persuade her to talk, *I* can."

"We do this my way," Frank said, his voice low, threatening.

The men tensed visibly. Abby stepped back, pulling Elena with her. Ramon touched the butt of the gun sticking out of the waistband of his pants, his eyes never leaving Frank's face.

"Your way will get us all killed," Frank said quietly.

Ramon stared at him for a long moment, his face motionless, then suddenly he smiled and shook his head. "Then I will go to the store myself. I'll bring food, and some beer and tequila. I need a drink." He ordered his men to stay and not let Frank and the woman and child out of their sights.

As Ramon left, Frank offered Abby the stool and turned to the men. "You're scaring the little girl," he said in Spanish. "Go outside. You can guard just as well from there."

With obvious reluctance, they moved out into a smaller courtyard than the one Frank had taken her to earlier. It looked as if someone had been camping in it. There was a fire pit in the center and some boxes that might have been pulled up for seats. Through the crumbling wall, Abby saw them sit down on the boxes, and watch sullenly from the darkness at the edge of the lantern light as the sky over Big Bend began to lighten.

Abby sat down on the stool, pulling Elena up into her arms, hugging her, wondering how Frank had gotten involved with these men and just who was in charge. Elena sucked on her thumb, something she still did when she was tired. Or scared. Or without Sweet Ana.

She thought she heard a noise in the distance. A faint buzzing sound. It seemed to be coming from behind the house. She looked at Frank and realized he was listening, too. She could almost feel him tense. Hadn't he said they didn't have much time?

"Do you know where the money is?" he whispered, still watching the men.

"No," she admitted quietly, suddenly on guard.

"I was afraid of that," he said, sounding genuinely sorry. There was no doubt; he'd been waiting for something. He now looked spring-loaded, like a diamondback rattler getting ready to strike.

Fear sent a shudder through her. "Frank, what—"

The sound of a helicopter suddenly filled the air. It rose up from the backside of the mountain and dropped down on them. *Whoop. Whoop. Whoop.* Then, suddenly, there was a blast of artillery fire.

Abby dove with Elena to the floor. She saw Frank draw his weapon. She scrambled to her feet and, shielding Elena, ran hunched-over down the hall, looking for a way out as bullets exploded behind her.

She heard Frank call out, his voice lost in the crack of gunfire and the steady whoop of helicopter blades hovering overhead.

JAKE HEARD the helicopter just as he reached the left side of the old mining building. The adobe structure sat against the mountainside overlooking Study Butte, the walls deteriorating, part of the roof gone, a dim light glowing from its center.

He thought he could make out two vehicles parked in some scrub brush off to the right and wondered how many men he'd find inside. He knew he wouldn't be able to handle many in his condition. His only hope was getting in the first shots, and that was mighty optimistic.

Then he heard the chopper. It rose up out of the darkness over the rough edge of the mountains silhouetted against the dawn sky. The large military helicopter crested the mountain and swooped down on the mining building like a giant wasp.

He ducked behind a wall as the big bird hovered over the center of what was left of the structure and started firing. Weapon drawn, he worked his way toward the rat-a-tat-tat of firearms, praying Abby and Elena weren't in there.

ABBY COULD HEAR footfalls on the broken tile floor behind her, but she didn't turn. She ran harder, seeing an opening ahead, the faint light of day bleeding through a pale gray. She hit the opening and burst through with Elena in her arms. Daybreak washed the rough mountains of Big Bend in quicksilver, but night's shadows still pooled, dark and cool, at the edges of the buildings hidden from daylight.

She didn't see the helicopter until it was almost on her. It came in a deafening roar of whirling dust and noise. Suddenly it was in front of her, hovering just above the ground. A dark figure leapt out. Before she could turn and run, strong arms grabbed Elena from her and swung the child up into the dark cavity of the chopper. Abby screamed, the sound lost in the whoop of the blades as she rushed the chopper. The dark figure jumped back inside, the helicopter started to rise.

Abby grabbed hold of the man's leg, struggling to see her child in the whirling dust, frantic to learn who had taken her, as she tried to pull herself up into the chopper.

A face came into focus just above her. It was the same man who'd pulled a gun on her on the train.

JAKE HAD SEEN Abby burst out of the building running, with Elena in her arms. He'd dashed toward her, knowing he wouldn't get to her in time. He'd called out, trying to warn her as he watched the helicopter swoop down on her and Elena. But he knew she hadn't heard him. The noise of the chopper drowned out everything but the erratic gunfire still coming from the mining building.

He ran, his heart thudding as his feet pounded the earth. Helplessly, he watched as someone jumped from the helicopter and grabbed Elena. All his attempts to assure himself that the chopper was the cavalry come to save Abby and Elena failed when a second man swung out the side and opened fire on him.

He got off one shot, then stopped, afraid he might hit Elena inside the aircraft. It was a lucky shot. The man tumbled off, hitting the ground in a puff of dust.

He ran all out, closer now, but not close enough. His head pounded harder than his boot soles. His vision blurred. A numbness seemed to wash through his limbs and just lifting his feet took all his energy.

As he reached the chopper, he saw that Abby had a death grip on the man's leg and was desperately trying to pull herself up into the chopper.

The aircraft started to lift off. He jumped up and grabbed onto the chopper's skids, his body swinging, making the craft wobble in the air. He looked up, unable to see the men inside, only the man's hand trying to loosen Abby's grasp on his leg.

For a moment, it looked as if the man would drag Abby up into the helicopter. Instead, he broke her hold on him. She dropped to the ground and into the dust storm a half dozen feet beneath the chopper.

With the last of his strength, Jake grabbed the undercarriage and tried to climb up into the helicopter. But a boot heel swung down on his hand, breaking his tenuous hold.

He fell, dropping hard into the dust, the fall knocking the air from his lungs. He lay in the dirt, gasping for breath, watching as the helicopter hovered for a moment overhead. Then the big bird was gone. With Elena inside it.

Chapter Twelve

"Elena!" Abby cried. "Elena! Oh God, no."

He pulled her to him, burying her face into his shoulder, searching for words of comfort, but he could find none. The bastards had taken his daughter.

"Oh, Jake," Abby cried. "I thought you were—"

"Yeah," he said grimacing. "Damned near."

He breathed in the scent of her, relishing the feel of her, holding on to her for dear life.

"I thought I'd never see you again," she whispered.

This was the second time he'd thought he'd never see *her* again. "I know what you mean." He gazed into her dark eyes as the sky over Big Bend lightened with the approaching sunrise.

"They took Elena," she said, her voice thick with tears.

He nodded and struggled to sit up. But who were *they,* anyway? And what the hell did they want? All this for the stolen drug money? He found that hard to believe.

"Are you sure you're all right?"

"Yeah," he lied, his heart breaking with worry over Elena. He could barely see and realized his gunshot wound had started bleeding again. He pressed his shirtsleeve to the bandage, and it came away wet and dark. Several shots echoed from the old mining office.

"This might be a good time to hit the road," he said, trying to keep his voice light. Trying hard to keep her from knowing just how worried he was about Elena. Or about their own chances of getting out of this.

She helped him up, supporting him, as she urged him toward one of the abandoned buildings just ahead of them.

He stumbled through the thin morning light spilling over the ghost town. The air around him felt too heavy, the dawn too bright, the buzzing in his ears too loud. He didn't know how much farther he could go.

She must have sensed his fatigue as she hustled him to the dark side of one of the ruins. "Let's stop for a minute." She let go of him and he dropped into the shadows, weak and dizzy and bone-chilling cold.

Abby knelt beside him, fear tightening her throat and making her heart ache. His bandage was soaked in fresh blood. She didn't know how badly he was hurt, but she knew he wasn't going far. Not on his feet, anyway.

She slipped to the edge of the building and glanced back up the hillside, memory playing again the horrible moments when Elena was pulled into the helicopter.

Elena. Oh God. Elena. Her tears tasted bitter and her aching heart labored in her chest. She had to get Jake out of here. Get him to a doctor. Then she could figure out what to do. If only she could remember her training. She'd never needed it more than she did right now.

She focused again on the large building set back against the mountainside. She didn't think anyone had followed them. But she couldn't be sure someone hadn't seen them, knew where they were and would be coming soon.

Several more shots drifted down from the hillside. Who was still up there, still exchanging volleys? She didn't even know who was fighting whom.

"We can't stay here," Jake whispered behind her.

"I know. Just for a few minutes." She went to him. "Until you catch your breath."

He smiled up at her, his fingers lifting to touch her cheek, tears welling in his eyes and in her own. She quickly touched her fingers to his lips and shook her head. If he even mentioned Elena, she would fall apart.

He kissed her fingers, his gaze understanding. "I found this hidden in Sweet Ana," he whispered as he dug something out of his pocket. He handed her a small key. "I want you to have it, just in case something happens to me."

"Nothing is going to happen to you." Oh God, how badly was he wounded? Did he know something she didn't? She stared at the key for a moment. It could be the key to getting Elena back. "You found it *inside* the doll?"

"The stitching was a different color and crudely sewn on that side of the cloth body," he said.

She closed the key in her fist, the sharp metal digging into her palm. Elena's lost doll. It had been lying beside Julio's dead body. "Julio was going to take Elena with him. He was planning to use her." And the doll. A man and his daughter looked less suspicious than a man traveling alone.

He started to get up. "I hid the Explorer behind the old church. If we could—"

"Are the keys in it?"

He nodded.

"Stay here, I'll be right back."

She left before he could argue, running along the shadowed sides of the buildings, keeping out of sight, until she reached the Explorer. She started it quickly and drove back to where she'd left Jake.

He'd gotten to his feet and stood propped against the adobe wall. She leaned over to shove open the passenger-side door. He slid in and slammed the door just as the glint of a chrome bumper appeared from behind a stand of brushy trees up on the mountainside. The vehicle came out of a cloud of dust, moving fast, headed her way.

She hit the gas, tires spinning in the dirt as she flipped a cookie. Dust rooster-tailed behind the Explorer, as she headed south toward the Rio Grande.

"I think you should know, Abby Diaz was one helluva driver, especially in this kind of situation," Jake said.

She glanced over at him, not at all sure that was true. He'd buckled his seat belt and was now leaning back into the seat, his eyes closed, his face ashen in the glow of the dash lights. "You'd better hope so."

She skidded onto Farm Route 170 headed west, the pavement disappearing under the hood in a blur, and looked back to see not one, but two vehicles in hot pursuit.

"Are you all right?" she asked, knowing if he'd been all right he'd have been driving.

He opened his eyes and gave her a wan smile. "Good enough."

The truth was, he felt light-headed, his pulse throbbing to the buzzing in his head, and he couldn't seem to keep his eyes open.

"Do you have any idea who that might be behind us?" she asked.

"Not a clue. At this point, I just figure *everyone* wants us dead. How about you?"

She shook her head. "Could be Frank. He's the one who took Elena and me from the house after you were shot."

"Jordan?"

"He was with some of Calderone's men, including possibly the man who killed Julio, a man named Ramon.''

Ramon Hernandez and Frank Jordan in Study Butte, working together. ''I was afraid Frank was involved when we got the report on you,'' he said quietly, cursing silently to himself. Frank.

''He swears he didn't have anything to do with what happened six years ago or my abduction by Julio. Nor does he admit he knew I was being held in Mexico,'' she said, sounding as disbelieving as he was.

His anger made him weaker, more worried for Elena, more worried for Abby. Frank had to be behind Elena's kidnapping, but he'd never seemed like the kind of agent who could be corrupted by mere money. The FBI had always been too important to him, his rise to the top and the power that came with that. What had changed?

He swore as he looked out at the road ahead. Just when he'd thought things couldn't get any worse, they were on the wrong road out of town!

He looked over at the speedometer, then back at the two cars on their butt. He closed his eyes again, no longer worried about his gunshot wound or his health. He'd never survive this car ride.

They flew through the town of Lajitas, an old army post built to protect this part of Texas from Pancho Villa. The irony didn't escape him, even in his weakened state. They raced through the frontier-style town with its plank sidewalks and hitching rails, the streets empty at this hour, the two pursuing vehicles staying right with them.

Jake wondered where the cops were. Probably in bed. He wished that was where he was. With Abby. With Elena just across the hall, sleeping peacefully. He squeezed his eyes tight, fighting the pain, fighting images of Elena, the feel of her small hand securely in his, the scent of lilac on her skin as he leaned down to kiss her good-night—

He opened his eyes at the sound of Abby's shocked curse. She'd reached El Camino del Rio, a fifty-mile stretch of pavement that wound like a dark and dangerous snake beside the Rio Grande from Lajitas to Presidio. The narrow blacktop twisted and turned up and down and around the volcanic and limestone rock formations of the Bofecillos Mountains, finally dumping out into the fertile river valley at Presidio.

If they were that lucky.

But there was no turning back. Not with whoever was right behind them.

"You've driven this road before," he told Abby, trying to sound confident and unconcerned. Driving the road going the speed limit in broad daylight was precarious. At close to a hundred miles an hour at first light, it was beyond dangerous. Add two carloads of probable killers and you had a very bad situation.

She shot him a look.

"Don't worry," he assured her. "You can handle this with your eyes closed."

"Right." She let out a small, scared laugh, but at least it was a laugh and he knew the old Abby Diaz was at the wheel. He felt a little better, a little more optimistic about their chances. At least Isabella Montenegro wasn't driving.

The route was the same one Pancho Villa used for his mule trains during the Mexican Revolution. He doubted it had changed much. Someone had just thrown a little blacktop on it and called it a scenic route.

Abby took the first hairpin curve with a determined look and a white-knuckled grip on the wheel. The Rio Grande stayed with them, quicksilver in the early light. So did the vehicles behind them.

He noticed that the first one, a green Dodge pickup, was gaining. Moving in for the kill? The way they were driving, they knew the road well. He'd figured their pursuers had been waiting for this hazardous stretch of highway to make their move.

The pickup came up fast behind them.

"Jake!" Abby cried.

He braced himself. The truck slammed into their back bumper. Metal crunched as they were thrown forward. But Abby kept the rig on the road.

"Never fear, darlin'," he said as he hurriedly rolled down his window. The early-morning air was already hot and scented with dust. He felt drunk, only running on a couple of cylinders, not all pistons firing. But he thought he could still shoot.

Unbuckling his seat belt, he leaned out the car window and fired back at the truck. The bullet made a clean entry into the windshield, leaving a web of white the size of his head in the glass but on the passenger side instead of the driver's. *Settle down.* The pickup backed off, but not fast enough. He fired again.

The left front tire exploded in a puff of gray smoke. The pickup began to rock, the front veering from side to side. Rock and roll. The truck took the ditch flying, smacked into the side of the mountain and disappeared in a rolling cloud of dust.

One down, he thought grimly. He flopped back into his seat, almost too weak to roll up the window.

Abby let out a breath. "Nice shooting."

"Thanks." He saw the second vehicle, a Chevy Suburban, come up fast in the side mirror. The gleam of a shotgun barrel came out the passenger-side window.

"Get down!" he yelled.

The blast shattered the rear window sending glass showering over the backseat. He swung around and fired through the gaping hole, putting one in the grill and doing only cosmetic damage to the hood with the second.

The Suburban roared up beside the Explorer. Another shotgun blast took out the back side window.

Jake swore as Abby took a curve on two wheels and for a moment he thought this would be it. *Adios.* He pulled up and fired as the Suburban dropped back only a little for the curve, then started to make another run at them.

The gun felt too heavy, his finger too weak on

the trigger, his vision blurred, the whole scene sur-real. But he got off another shot, then another. The Suburban was too close to take out a tire. It moved up the left side of them again. The barrel of the shotgun glinted dully in the dawn as it leveled at Abby.

He threw himself over the back of the seat and emptied the clip through the missing side window. The man with the shotgun saw it coming and ducked, but the driver didn't. He slumped over the wheel as one shot hit home.

The man with the shotgun came up again, un-aware that his driver had been hit. Abby went into a tight right-hand curve. The Suburban left the road going over eighty. But not before the man with the shotgun got off one last blast.

The shot was off-center. It peppered Abby's door with buckshot and got just enough of Abby's side window to shatter it. Glass showered over both of them.

"Are you all right?" Jake cried.

She didn't answer, the Explorer rocking as she fought the wheel.

"Abby?"

"Yeah," she said finally, after she got it back under control. Behind them, the Suburban had dropped off the side of the mountain and was now cartwheeling toward the river.

Abby topped a hill and they dropped down into the farming community of Redford with its collec-tion of adobe and wood-frame houses. A church, the

Redford Co-op Goat Cheese Factory and the Cordera Store blurred past, seeming too normal.

Abby slowed the Explorer. He crawled back into the front seat, buckled up again and took a deep breath, no longer feeling much of anything. Abby didn't say a word. He watched the side mirror, but no other vehicles appeared. It wasn't over and he knew Abby was more than aware of that. It wouldn't be over until they got their little girl back. And they *would* get her back. He wouldn't let himself think anything else. Couldn't.

He felt sick, more tired than he'd ever remembered being, and cold, as if his body had caught fire and was burning from the inside out.

They rolled into Presidio as the sun rose over the tops of the rugged mountains. The "Hottest Town in Texas" was just waking as they drove in. Across the border, Ojinaga, its Mexican sister city, dozed in the sunshine.

"Neuvo Real Presidio de Nuestra Senora de Betlena y Santiago de Las Amarillas de La Junta de Los Rios Norte y Conchos," he said, then singsang the words like a mantra, feeling oddly light as if he were floating. Or drunk.

Abby looked over at him and frowned. "New Royal Garrison of Our Lady of Bethlehem and St. James on the Banks of the Junction of the Rio Grand and Conchos Rivers?"

He nodded. "Wonder why they shortened it to Presidio? Just doesn't have the same ring, does it?" His gaze fell on her and he smiled. It felt crooked even to his lips. "You are one hell of a woman behind a wheel. I take back everything I ever said about your driving." He laughed. It sounded to his ears as if he were down in a well. "You are one hell of a woman."

"Are you sure you're all right?" he heard her ask from a distance. She reached across the seat to touch his forehead. "Jake, you're freezing."

He laughed. At least he thought he did. It had a carnival-midway feel to it inside his head. Then he remembered something. "Abby, there's something I should have told—" He lost the thought as he lost consciousness.

HIS TANNED, square-jawed, handsome face was pale against the white hospital sheets. He opened his eyes. They'd never looked more green. Never looked more like Elena's, she thought, with a stab of pain.

She smiled down at him. "How ya doin'?"

He returned her smile. "You tell me."

"Just fine," she said softly as she brushed a dark lock of hair back from his forehead. He felt warm. But he'd lost a lot of blood. "Looks like you might make it."

"Good." He started to get up. "Let's get out of here, then."

She pushed him back onto the bed easily and pulled up a chair beside him, holding his hand in hers. "You're not going anywhere. Doctor's orders." He started to argue. "I'm serious, Jake.

You've got to get your strength back. They just want to keep you overnight and get some fluids in you.''

"Elena—"

"There isn't anything we can do until we get you well." She lowered her voice, although only the two of them were in the room. "Or until we hear from the kidnappers."

"Yeah." He frowned as he glanced toward the window. It was afternoon. He'd slept all morning. "You haven't heard anything yet?"

She shook her head. Like him, she'd thought they'd have called by now. She'd taken Jake to the safest hospital she could find, a small private one outside of town. Then she'd waited, praying he'd be all right, praying the kidnappers would call.

She'd just assumed they had Jake's cell-phone number because of Frank. She couldn't bear to think the kidnappers had no way of contacting them.

"I still can't understand how they found us," Jake said.

She recalled his words: *If we aren't safe here, then we're not safe anywhere.* "If you can't trust the Feds, then who can you trust?" she said.

Why hadn't they called? It scared her. Who had her daughter? And what did they want?

The obvious answer was the stolen drug money. So why did she think there had to be more to it?

"This morning reminded me of when the two of us used to work together," Jake said.

She nodded, wishing she could remember. "My memory is starting to come back," she told him, disturbed by the bits and pieces she kept seeing in her mind's eye. Some memories made no sense but left her anxious and worried, as if they were important things she desperately needed to remember. Jake was hurt and someone had their little girl. That was all she knew for sure.

"The harder I try to remember that night, the less clear anything is," she told him.

"There's no reason for you to remember that night," Jake said quickly, squeezing her hand. "Forget the past, Abby. All that matters now is the future."

She wished that were true. But she couldn't throw off the feeling that the answer to everything that was happening now was hidden in her past.

"It's funny, I keep thinking I remember you and me arguing about something the afternoon before," she said, confused by a glimpse of memory. "I just feel like something happened, something I need to remember."

He shook his head slowly and reached up to cup her cheek in his large palm, his thumb moving in slow circles, caressing her skin. "It was a stupid fight. But believe me, it didn't have anything to do with what's happening now."

She studied him, concerned he was holding something back. But why? "What about?"

He glanced away for a moment. "Dell Harper."

"Dell?"

He took a breath and let it out slowly. "Like I said, it was a stupid fight. I just felt that you were being too protective of him and that it was affecting your work.'' He met her gaze. ''I was a little…jealous, too.''

She wondered about her relationship with Dell. Did Jake have anything to be jealous of? She tried to pull up an image of Dell. A feeling. Nothing came.

''Is that what you were going to tell me earlier?'' she asked. ''About our fight?''

He nodded. ''Not that it has anything to do with what happened later.''

The nurse came in and told Abby she'd have to leave, the patient needed his rest. Before Jake could protest, the nurse gave him a shot.

''You'll be here when I wake up?'' he asked, already sounding groggy.

She nodded. ''You get better,'' she said and slipped a gun under his pillow when the nurse wasn't watching.

He smiled up at her, acknowledging the weapon and his possible need for it. ''Abby, I— Just watch your back.''

''Rest. I'll be fine.'' As she let go of his hand, she felt a sense of loss. For a moment, she almost changed her plans. The doctor had told her Jake would sleep through the night and she should get some rest. Rest was the last thing on her mind.

She'd seen to it that the doctor's report of the gunshot wound would never reach its destination. Not that she could see any reason why the men who had Elena would be searching for her and Jake. But even if they were, and even if they suspected how badly Jake was hurt and checked local hospitals, they wouldn't find a patient listed by the name of Jake Cantrell.

THE MOMENT the hospital-room door closed behind Abby, Jake thought about their argument six years ago. Looking back, it had been foolish. He'd been foolish. Arguing over Dell Harper.

He wished he'd never said anything to her. But the fact was, he'd been jealous of Dell and her friendship with him. Abby had been overly protective of the young FBI agent and Dell—well, Dell had always seemed too...interested in Abby.

But Jake still wished he'd kept it to himself. He'd regretted their argument for six years. In the end, a man's biggest regrets in life would involve a woman, he thought. He already had his share when it came to Abby.

Dell Harper was dead. Gone. He needed to concentrate on getting Elena back. On getting Abby to trust him again.

But at the back of his mind something warned him that he'd just made a terrible mistake. One he would live to more than regret.

Chapter Thirteen

On the drive to El Paso in the rental car, Abby pooled together everything she could remember and waded through it. Only a few fragmented memories remained from the day of the explosion, just enough to make her feel troubled and tense. She could sense something important buried deep in her memory. Her subconscious teased her with it, holding it just out of reach.

Was it as the doctors at the hospital had told her six years ago, something she'd repressed because she couldn't face it? Whatever it was, the harder she tried to remember, the more it evaded her.

Beside her on the seat was Sweet Ana, the cell phone the FBI had given Jake and the envelope she'd found under Julio's body. Just the sight of the doll made her cry, but she wiped at her tears, stubbornly determined to find her daughter and put the cherished doll back into the child's arms, just as she would take her daughter in hers.

Under her jacket, she wore Jake's shoulder holster

with the gun she'd taken from one of Calderone's men at the border. When had that been? It seemed like a lifetime ago.

She wished the phone would ring. That the kidnappers would call and name their price. But she didn't sit around and wait. She couldn't.

She drove into El Paso in the early afternoon. El Paso was a big sprawling city with a combination of cultures that made her very aware that Mexico was just across the border. It reminded her of her own Spanish heritage. At a convenience store, she asked for directions to the El Paso Central bus station.

She found it easily but drove around the block several times before she parked. She didn't think she'd been followed—at least not that she'd seen, and she'd been watching closely.

Her instincts told her that no one would be waiting here for her, either. If they knew where the money was stashed, they wouldn't have kidnapped her daughter. But still, she felt the hair rise on the back of her neck, her skin prickle with apprehension, as she walked into the large bus terminal.

According to the schedule, the bus to San Antonio had just left and buses going to Albuquerque and Phoenix wouldn't be leaving for a few hours.

Passengers loitered in the lobby, some standing around looking restless, others mesmerized by the large TV mounted on the wall. A few, probably waiting for even later buses, dozed on the uncomfortable chairs or curled up on the floor.

She walked through the throng toward the back of the building, following the sign that read Rest Rooms to the row of old beat-up green metal lockers. As she walked, she searched the faces of the people she passed.

She didn't see anyone she knew. Or at least anyone she recognized. That was one of the real drawbacks of amnesia, she thought.

She felt edgy, even with the reassuring feel of the gun against her ribs, as she wandered through the rows of lockers. A few passengers or possibly homeless people slept at the ends of the rows, as unrecognizable as bundles of clothing. Any of them could be staking out locker No. 17, waiting on her to show with the key.

But one good look at the lockers themselves and she knew no one would sleep in a huddle on a bus-station floor to wait for her to open a door that the most amateur crook could crack with a hairpin in a matter of seconds.

The thought did settle her down some as she walked to locker No. 17. She stood looking at it for signs that the lock had been tampered with. Even after a half dozen coats of dark green paint, the metal locker front was dented and scratched, banged-up and defaced, but the lock looked fine.

She dug into her jeans, glancing around. No one seemed the least bit interested and yet she felt as if she was being watched. She waited a few moments, then pulled out the key and tried it in the lock. She turned it, heard a click and felt the door give. One thought struck her: what man in his right mind would put several million dollars in a bus locker? Would that much money even fit in a locker this size?

But then she still couldn't imagine Julio stealing that much from Calderone.

She swung the door open and stared into the shadowy darkness of the locker, instantly surprised by how empty it was. Cautiously, as if she thought there was a diamondback rattler coiled inside, she reached in.

The money was stacked in the back, each bundle of bills fastened with a rubber band. Without pulling it out, she thumbed through one. All used hundreds in U.S. dollars. The bundle was a good three inches thick or more, so she knew it had to be more than ten thousand dollars.

Hurriedly she thumbed through several more, then quickly estimated the number of bundles. Just over three hundred thousand dollars. Definitely nowhere near millions.

So where was the rest of the money? Maybe he'd hidden it in a variety of places, just in case he had any trouble getting to one of his stashes. Or maybe this was all there was.

From inside her jacket, she took out two brown shopping bags and began to slide the money into the largest of the two, watching out of the corner of her eye for movement.

But as she filled the bag, no one approached. No one even seemed to pay her any mind. She slid the last wad of money into the bag, then covered the bundles of bills with the second bag, and felt around in the locker to make sure she'd gotten it all.

Her fingers brushed over a scrap of paper. A note reminding Julio where he'd left the rest of the money? Not likely. She withdrew a folded piece of newsprint, yellowed and ragged. Unfolding it, she saw that it was nothing more than a clipping torn from the Houston Chronicle, and she almost put it back without even looking at, thinking it had been left by a previous renter. But three letters in the headline caught her eye. *FBI.*

Bystander Dies in FBI Raid. She glanced at the publication date. Almost twenty years ago. Surely this couldn't have anything to do with—a name leapt out of the copy. Frank Jordan. Then a name Jake had mentioned to her. Hal ''Buster'' Mc-Norton. The man who'd died six years ago in the same routine investigation Abby herself had almost died in.

She stared at the photo. So faded and worn, it was impossible to make out the faces, but it appeared to be of a man beside a body on the ground in front of a restaurant. She could almost make out the neon sign reflected in the plate-glass window out front.

She heard someone approaching and quickly stuffed the newspaper article into her bag, raked a hand over the rusted bottom of the inside of the locker to make sure she'd gotten everything, then locked it again.

It was hard to walk slowly out of the bus terminal.

Harder still not to look over her shoulder. But somehow, she did it.

When she reached her car, she tossed the bag onto the floor on the passenger side, got in and locked the doors. She desperately wanted to look more closely at the newspaper clipping, but she started the car and slipped into the traffic, watching behind her.

After driving for twenty minutes in an ever-widening circle, she pulled into a fast-food drive-through and ordered a large coffee. She realized she hadn't eaten all day, and amended her order to include a cheeseburger and fries.

With her coffee and food, she parked in the lot where she could watch the street and dug out the newspaper clipping again and turned on the dome light. She read it as she ate.

The article was pretty straightforward. The FBI had raided a business believed to be manufacturing cocaine. During the chase that ensued, a young woman bystander was killed. Her name was being withheld until notification of relatives. FBI agent Frank Jordan refused to comment on the raid or the death of the bystander.

She reached into the bag and finished off the last of the fries, not even aware that she'd eaten all of her burger. Downing the last of the coffee, she studied the photo again, wondering what this article could possibly have to do with Julio and the money she'd found.

It probably didn't. But she also didn't believe that it just happened to be in the bottom of the locker, not the way it had been carefully ripped from the paper and folded. Or the fact that the newspaper clipping was almost twenty years old. Or that the article just happened to mention Frank Jordan. And Buster McNorton.

Too many coincidences.

Then she saw something that made her heart pound. The byline. The article had been written by Crystal Winfrey. Had Crystal Jordan been a newspaper woman before she became a TV anchorwoman? Before she married Frank Jordan? It seemed likely.

Was she still an anchorwoman for a San Antonio television news station? Or had she gone on to something else in the last six years?

She made a few calls on the cell phone and found Crystal working for a small, obscure public TV station in Houston. The former anchorwoman now worked behind the camera on the night shift. For a few minutes she sat in the parking lot trying to talk herself out of it. When she called Jake, the nurse told her he was sleeping, his condition improved.

She'd thought about calling Crystal. But she wasn't sure Crystal would talk to her. She wasn't even sure what she hoped to accomplish by contacting Crystal in the first place.

But the newspaper clipping nagged at her. It had to have some significance, and Crystal Winfrey Jordan was her only lead. And Abby wanted to surprise her.

All the way to the airport she told herself this was

nothing more than a wild-goose chase. Worse, she wouldn't be able to get a call from the kidnappers during the short flight. But thirty minutes later she was on a jet winging its way across Texas, trying desperately not to think about Elena and the man who had her or about Jake. Trying to think like an FBI agent. Not a mother. Not a lover.

As ABBY GOT out of her car, locked it and headed toward the TV station, she felt again as if someone was watching her. But she hadn't seen anyone on the flight who looked familiar and the station parking lot was half-empty, with no one hanging around.

The television station was quiet in the office area, away from the action of live broadcasting. Her footsteps echoed down the long, windowless hallway.

"Excuse me," she said, sticking her head into the open doorway of the broom-closet-sized office marked Jordan.

The woman behind the desk looked up and Abby remembered her.

Crystal Jordan had once been a beautiful woman. Tall, lean and blond, with a dynamite face that flirted with the camera and a smile that radiated honesty on the screen.

But that was not the woman now sitting behind the cluttered desk at the end of the hallway.

"Yes?" she asked. Her hair was still blond, bleached thin. It hung straight to her shoulders, a style too young for the face it framed. It was a wrinkled, sallow face, the face and voice of a woman who'd spent too much time on a barstool, trying to kill herself with booze and cigarettes. "Can I help you?"

But there was something familiar about that voice, a familiarity that struck a chord with her. She'd once considered Crystal a friend. "Crystal," she said softly. "It's me, Abby. Abby Diaz."

Crystal picked up a pair of glasses from the desk. As she hurriedly settled them on her nose, she jerked back, eyes wide, an expression that held both surprise and fear on her face. And in that instant, Abby wondered how long Crystal Winfrey Jordan had known she was alive.

Crystal got awkwardly to her feet. "My God, it *is* you."

Abby closed the door behind her and leaned against it. "When did Frank tell you I was alive?"

The older woman stepped back. "Frank and I are divorced. He doesn't tell me—"

"Don't lie to me, Crystal. I've been a prisoner in Mexico for six long years, my daughter's been kidnapped and someone is trying to kill me. I'm not in the mood for any more lies. You knew I was alive. You knew I'd be coming here. Why is that?"

Crystal reached for her intercom, but Abby jerked it out of her hand, ripping it from the wall and tossing it into the corner. She did the same with the phone, knocking the piles of papers on the desk to the floor.

The former anchorwoman wobbled for a moment

on her high heels, then dropped into the chair behind the desk again. "What do you want from me?"

"The truth," Abby snapped.

Crystal looked as if she might cry, but she no longer appeared fearful, just resigned. "Frank told me a couple of days ago. He was in shock. He couldn't believe it."

Abby just bet he *was* in shock.

She pulled the folded newspaper clipping from her jacket pocket. Unfolding the yellowed paper, she laid it on the desk. "Do you remember this?"

Crystal drew the clipping closer. "Where did you get it?"

"I found it in a bus-station locker with three hundred thousand dollars of stolen drug money."

The older woman paled under the fluorescent lighting and her fingers trembled as she shrank back from the newspaper clipping.

"Frank was the one who shot the bystander, wasn't he?" Abby said, voicing what she'd suspected from the moment she'd read it.

Crystal nodded. "It was an accident. She was just a kid. Maybe sixteen. Pretty little thing. Frank never got over it."

"Who is that in the photo, leaning over her?" Something about the blurry figure looked almost familiar to Abby although his face was hidden.

"Her boyfriend. He was hysterical. I felt so sorry for him."

"Do you remember his name?"

Crystal shook her head. "It's been years."

"What about the girl's name?"

Again the newswoman couldn't recall.

Abby folded the newspaper clipping. Frank had shot the bystander. But what did that have to do with anything? What did the clipping have to do with Julio? With the stolen drug money? With getting her daughter back?

She watched Crystal pull out a drawer in her desk, knowing instinctively the woman wasn't reaching for a weapon. Crystal dug out a pint of vodka and poured two fingers into her dirty coffee cup.

"You know, I always envied you," the older woman said. "You had everything I wanted."

Abby watched her in surprise, wondering how a woman like Crystal Winfrey Jordan could have wanted for anything back in her heyday.

"You had Frank's respect," Crystal said, lifting the cup in a mocking toast. She downed the clear liquid without a blink and licked her lips. "I used to think he was half in love with you."

The words hit Abby like ice water. She shivered in the confined, hot room. She'd seen Frank as a mentor. Surely Crystal couldn't mean that he'd had a romantic interest in her.

Crystal poured herself another drink and downed it. "I do remember the name of the barbecue place, now that I think of it. The girl worked there, was a good friend of the family. It was called H's Second Avenue Barbecue." Crystal seemed to focus on Abby. "But what does this have to do with getting your daughter back?"

"I'm not sure it does," she admitted, hating to think she'd wasted her time coming here.

Crystal looked up at her, tears welling in her eyes.

Abby felt the old kinship, a remembered closeness with this woman. "Frank's involved with a drug lord name Tomaso Calderone and he or Calderone's men have my daughter."

Crystal shook her head. "Not Frank."

"Maybe you don't know him as well as you think." But she could see that Crystal didn't believe it. The woman was still in love with her ex-husband. Love was blind and deaf, it appeared.

"I'm sorry about what happened to you, but Frank would never have hurt you," Crystal said. "Nor your little girl."

"I'm sure he didn't know I was alive in Mexico these past six years either." Abby wrote down the cell phone number on a scrap of paper and laid it on the desk. "If you hear *anything* about my daughter, will you call me?"

Crystal's faded blue eyes welled again with tears. "Frank doesn't have your daughter, Abby. He's in intensive care in a hospital in San Antonio. He's not expected to live. He was shot trying to save you and your daughter."

Chapter Fourteen

With her flight not leaving for several hours and still stunned by what Crystal had told her, Abby drove around Houston, feeling lost. She kept thinking back to last night, replaying Frank's words in the dilapidated building in Study Butte. Searching for the key to finding Elena. He'd wanted to know where the money was. Said it was the only way she could save her life and Elena's. She'd gotten the impression he'd been expecting someone. He'd said she was wasting valuable time. But had he been expecting the men in the helicopter? The men who had taken Elena?

What bothered her most was that Frank might have been trying to save her and Elena. Was that possible? She'd heard shots behind her and Elena as she fled, but she couldn't be sure Frank had been shooting at her. Nor could she explain what he'd been doing with Calderone's men.

She called the Presidio hospital on the cell phone from her car, hoping to talk to Jake but the nurse said he was still out, sleeping peacefully and still improving.

Relieved he was better, she hung up and sat for a moment looking out into the darkness. It had been easier, thinking Frank was behind the kidnapping. But if he wasn't, then who had her daughter? And why hadn't they called?

She tried calling the hospital in San Antonio but couldn't even find out if Frank Jordan was a patient.

Bereft and more frightened than she wanted to admit, she dialed directory assistance, desperately needing something to occupy her mind—and the time—before her flight.

Surprisingly, H's Second Avenue Barbecue was still in business after all these years. Like many Texas barbecue joints, it was small, nondescript and out-of-the-way. She smelled the meat cooking over the hickory as she got out of her car. There were only a few tables and half a dozen stools at a counter, most empty this time of the night.

She sat down at the counter and opened the menu, looking the place over before she settled on a barbecued pork sandwich and a cola.

As a young waitress wearing the name tag Jennifer took her order, she noticed the framed photographs on the walls, some of them quite old. She studied one—a picture of two people holding large platters of food.

She got up for a closer look. "Who are these people?" she asked as Jennifer rushed by.

"The original owners." The girl carried two huge

plates of barbecued pork ribs that smelled wonderful as they passed. "The Harpers," she added over her shoulder.

Harper? She told herself there had to be thousands of Harpers in the country as she sat down again. When Jennifer brought her sandwich and cola, she asked, "Did they have a son named Dell Harper by any chance?"

She could tell immediately the girl was too young to know, but an older waitress had overheard and came over. "You knew Dell?" Her name tag said she was Suzie.

"Maybe. Was he with the FBI?"

"Unfortunately." Suzie pulled down one of the photos from the wall and walked over to where Abby was sitting. She used the hem of her uniform top to clean the glass.

"Dell was a friend of mine," Abby said, recalling what Jake had told her, wishing she could remember Dell. "I used to be an FBI agent in the same division."

"The FBI did nothing but hurt Dell," the woman said bitterly. "First his girlfriend was killed. Then Dell, dying like he did." She wagged her gray head. "Pretty near destroyed that family. Bud and Lenore sold the place and left. Couldn't blame them."

"It was *Dell's* girlfriend who was shot by an FBI agent out front?" Abby repeated, her heart thudding.

The woman nodded. In the back, the cook called out "Order up," and the waitress handed her the framed photograph as she hurried to the kitchen.

She looked down into the faces. A smiling couple in their forties, a tall, lean young boy of about eleven standing with them. All three held platters of barbecued ribs in front of them.

She stared at the boy's face and felt a small nudge of memory. A prickling feeling of warmth and fondness, almost a memory. And something else. Something darker, colder, more frightening.

If she and Dell had really been close, then he must have told her about losing his girlfriend. She felt a ripple of apprehension crawl up her spine. What a coincidence that Dell ended up working for the man who'd killed his girlfriend. If you believed in coincidence.

Suzie came back and put the photograph on the wall again without a word.

Abby took a bite of her barbecued pork sandwich out of politeness. She no longer felt the least bit hungry, even though the barbecue was delicious. Why on earth had Dell gone into the FBI after what had happened to his girlfriend? How had he ended up working under Frank Jordan? And what was the clipping doing in the bus-station locker?

She feared none of it had anything to do with Elena's kidnapping. Dell Harper was dead. He'd died in the explosion that had almost killed her and *had* killed Buster McNorton. With a start, she realized that Buster McNorton was the other agent who'd been on the scene when Dell Harper's girlfriend was killed. Now Buster was dead, as well.

She put down the half-eaten sandwich, paid her

bill, leaving a good tip, and started out of the restaurant, her heart pounding. She couldn't wait to get back to Jake.

But near the door, she spotted another photograph. Her footsteps slowed. She stared at the smiling faces. Bud and Lenore Harper with their son Dell and another young man. The two boys wore baseball uniforms.

She grabbed Suzie's arm as the older woman was going past. "Is that another Harper son?" she asked, her heart a deafening drum in her ears.

"No, Dell was their only child."

"Then who—" She pointed at the second young man in the photograph.

"That was Dell's best friend, Tommy Barnett. The two grew up here in the neighborhood."

Abby swallowed. "Does he still live around here? Or have family?"

Suzie shook her head. "The Harpers *were* his family. The boy lived with an old-maid aunt who died years back, but he spent all of his time here with Dell." She studied the photograph for a moment and smiled. "Tommy idolized Dell. Did whatever Dell did. If Dell jumped off the roof, then Tommy did. Lenore called him Dell's shadow, always following Dell around like a puppydog."

She dragged her eyes from the photo, her gaze hardening as it settled on Abby. "Tommy always did what Dell did. He would have joined the FBI too, but couldn't get in. Probably doesn't know how lucky he is."

Abby stared at the photo of Dell Harper and his best friend, Tommy Barnett, the man who'd held her at gunpoint on the train, the man who'd kidnapped her daughter.

JAKE WOKE with a start and looked around the room, confused for a few moments, before he remembered where he was. The hospital room was empty. No Abby. His heart pounded furiously in his chest and he felt weak with fear. Hurriedly he buzzed the nurse.

"Yes?" she said, a dark silhouette in the doorway. He realized it was dark outside. How many hours had he been asleep? How long had it been since he'd seen Abby? His fear heightened. "Would you get Abby, my—"

"Your wife isn't here, Mr. Cooper." His wife? Mr. Cooper? He blinked. Of course Abby would have been too smart to admit him under his own name. And only a wife could come and go freely.

"Did my wife say where she was going?" he asked, his throat dry, his heart thudding in his chest.

"She left earlier. She called a few minutes ago to check on you and we told her you were sleeping peacefully. I'm sure she'll be here soon."

But he knew better. He knew Abby. And now that he felt stronger, his head clearer, he had a feeling he knew where she'd gone. After the money, so she'd be ready when the kidnappers called. But they wouldn't be calling. "She didn't say where she was?"

''No, but earlier she did ask where she could rent a car, and she left her cell-phone number, in case we needed to contact her. Try to get some more rest. I'm sure she'll be here soon.'' She closed the door.

Jake reached for the phone beside the bed and hurriedly dialed the cell-phone number, scared sick for Abby. He knew now how Frank had tracked him to Study Butte. The same way, he feared, Abby was being tracked right at this very moment.

AT THE DOOR of the restaurant, Abby hesitated. She looked out into the growing darkness and knew Tommy Barnett was out there somewhere. She'd felt his presence before El Paso. Except now, she knew who he was. She knew who had her daughter, who'd led her here. She just didn't know why.

The door opened and a couple came in, bringing with them the warm evening air. She looked past them to the pockets of darkness pooling in the parking lot and stepped back. Not yet.

Turning, she made her way to the ladies' rest room. It was vacant. Inside, she locked the door and reached into her purse for the cell phone.

She dialed the FBI number, not even realizing that she'd remembered it until her fingers had tapped out the once-so-familiar digits. She asked for Reese Ramsey, said it was urgent and waited as her call was transferred.

Reese came on the line, a little groggy, but he woke up quickly when she told him who she was.

"Abby Diaz is dead," he said, sounding suspicious.

"Guess again."

"Yeah? Well I have two reports that say otherwise."

Just the sound of his voice brought back a memory, crystal clear. "How about that party at Frank's when you got drunk and confessed to me your deepest darkest secrets on the back steps?"

Silence. "ABBY?"

"Tommy Barnett. I need to know everything you have on him." She waited for him to boot up his laptop.

If only she could remember what'd happened six years ago. If she was right and Dell was the one who'd tipped off Calderone to try to get Frank, then why was Frank still alive and Dell dead? And why did his best friend now have her daughter? If Crystal had told the truth and Frank Jordan was on his deathbed, what more did Tommy want? The money?

"Sorry," Reese said after a few minutes. "No Tommy Barnett."

"Are you sure? Keep in mind that according to the FBI, I'm dead."

"Look, Frank gave me the results of those tests himself. Take it up with him," Reese said. "Hold on, I've got your boy. Yep. He tried to get into the FBI, but failed psychological testing."

She gripped the phone tighter. Nutcase. A nutcase had her daughter.

"Oh boy. I just ran his name through the crime computer. He did three of fifteen in a Texas prison."

She caught her breath. "What was he in for?"

"Selling illegal substances. And Tommy was no small-time operator either."

Drugs? Conceivably Tommy could have found out about her and Elena from Julio. They *were* in the same business. Maybe even associates.

"Is Jake there with you?"

"He can't come to the phone right now," she lied, not sure why. But she knew she wasn't telling anyone where Jake was. Not even someone Jake trusted. "Thanks for the information." She hung up, her fingers shaking. What kind of man had Elena? She didn't want to think.

Someone knocked at the bathroom door. She knew she couldn't stay here. She thought about calling the police, but couldn't risk it. Tommy Barnett had Elena. And she thought she knew what he wanted. Eventually she'd have to deal with him if she hoped to get her daughter back.

She opened the bathroom door, half expecting to see him waiting for her. A small gray-haired elderly woman gave her a smile as she hurried into the rest room and closed the door behind her, leaving Abby standing outside in the hallway.

She walked through the restaurant toward the front door, studying the patrons out of the corner of her eye. No Tommy Barnett. No, he'd be waiting for her outside.

But as she walked to her car she saw no one, and

yet she swore she could feel him out there, watching her, waiting. Waiting for what?

She opened her car door, her fingers trembling, and climbed in, locking the door behind her. The cell phone rang, startling her. Tommy? Or Reese trying to reach Jake?

"Abby." The sound of Jake's voice brought tears to her eyes. "Where are you?"

"Houston. Jake, are you all right? I—"

"Abby, listen. I know how they found us in Study Butte. It's the cell phone. There must be a tracking device in it."

She stared at the phone in her hands, realization making her heart pound harder.

"You have to get rid of it, and quick. Frank—"

"It's not Frank, Jake. A man named Tommy Barnett has Elena. He was a friend of Dell Har—"

Her words were lost in an explosion of glass as her side window imploded. The cell phone was jerked from her hand. She turned and saw the familiar face just before she felt the blow.

Chapter Fifteen

"Abby!" Jake heard the glass break, heard her cry out, then a loud thunk came over the receiver as if the phone had been dropped to the pavement. He listened to the deadly silence, his heart slamming against his chest as he heard another sound. Abby being dragged from the car. A car door opened, then slammed closed. An engine revved, then faded away. He thought he'd die. He closed his eyes, squeezing the phone in his hand. Not again. God, please, don't let me lose her, not again.

Houston. She'd said she was in Houston. What the hell was she doing there? He couldn't imagine. Something to do with Dell Harper and another man he'd never heard of. Tommy Barnett. He realized he was still listening. At first all he heard was silence. Then he picked up another sound. It took him a moment to realize it was the loudspeaker coming from a ballpark. A baseball game! He could hear the crowd now.

He listened, concentrating hard. *Give me a name.*

Give me just one team name. Then he heard it. The Texas Red Devils were up by three.

He hung up and called Reese.

"I thought you were Abby calling back," Reese said.

"Abby called you?"

"Yeah, she's alive."

He only hoped.

"She needed me to run a name through the computer," Reese was saying. "Tommy Barnett."

"Who is he?"

"A pretty big-time drug dealer here in Houston."

Great. "Any connection to Dell Harper?"

"Not that I know of," Reese said, sounding surprised.

Dell was dead and had been for six years. What could it matter now anyway? "Listen, I need a jet. I need to get to Houston and quick. You can fill me in when you meet me at the airport. We've got to find Abby before it's too late." If it wasn't already.

Abby had said it wasn't Frank. Then why would he falsify the reports to make her look dead? Why would he be working with Ramon Hernandez? "Just hurry." He hung up and slipped out of bed to dress. He felt stronger. Or maybe he just told himself he did. Either way he was going after Abby.

THE WORLD came back slightly out of focus. In the fuzzy grayness, Abby remembered. It all came back fast and furious. Scenes racing through her mind, conversations, the past flooding her memory.

She was outside the warehouse in the darkness, waiting with Jake, her weapon drawn. When she looked down the side of the building, she saw Dell and her heart leapt into her throat. Had she really seen him signal someone out in the darkness?

Buster and Dell disappeared inside the warehouse. She followed, a terrible feeling taking possession of her. Dell hadn't been himself lately but he wouldn't talk about what was bothering him.

She slipped through the side door behind the two agents and stopped to let her eyes adjust to the semi-darkness. The warehouse was large and full of wooden crates. The air smelled musty and dank. Only a dim light burned near the center. She crouched behind a stack of crates for a moment, then moved toward the light and the sound of whispered voices.

As she neared, she realized Dell was talking with someone. Whoever it was, it wasn't Buster.

"You aren't changing your mind now," a male voice snapped. "We've worked too hard. Think of Amy."

"Amy's dead, Tee." Dell sounded weary.

She edged closer.

"If you don't have the stomach for this, I can do it for you."

"No, I can handle it," Dell said. "Let's just get it finished. Your part ready? Then you'd better get out of here. They'll be coming in any minute."

Oh God. What kind of trouble was Dell in? Finish what? She slipped to the edge of the crate and *peered around the corner. Her heart caught in her throat.*

Buster lay sprawled on the warehouse floor. Dell stood over him with another man, both with their backs to her. Dell had his weapon drawn and didn't seem to even notice Buster's body beside him. No, Dell wouldn't— No!

"Make it look good," Tee said, handing Dell a large clear plastic bag filled with white powder. Then Tee turned and disappeared between two crates.

She felt the hair on her neck rise. She rose to her feet and stepped out, gripping her weapon as she pointed it at her friend. "Dell, tell me Buster isn't dead. Tell me you didn't kill him."

Dell turned slowly.

The memory jerked to a halt, then began again in slow motion.

She could feel tears burn her eyes. Her legs felt weak, the gun in her hand too heavy and awkward. "Dell?" Her voice came out a whispered plea. She could hear the others coming. They'd be here any minute.

"I'm sorry, Abby. You and Frank are next." He raised his weapon, aiming it right at her.

No!

She saw herself dive to the floor and roll and come up firing. A trained reaction. Instinctive. She felt Dell's shot whiz past her head, too shocked to even realize how close he'd come to killing her. She saw him take the hits as her finger squeezed off the shots. One in the neck just above his bulletproof vest. The other snapping his head back as he went down.

She watched as if underwater, everything surreal, everything happening in microseconds, nothing making any sense. Someone grabbed her, pulled her back, struggling to get the weapon out of her hand. She fought him off and ran toward the sound of Jake's voice calling to her.

The building exploded around her. Flames and fire. Someone dragging her out, wrapping her in a rough, smelly fabric. Someone she didn't know. Pain. Terrible, terrible pain. Then darkness.

She blinked and swallowed. She'd killed Dell. Oh God. She squeezed her eyes shut. No wonder she hadn't been able to remember. No wonder. Her heart ached as she recalled how close she and Dell had been. Like the little brother she'd never had. She'd loved Dell.

She opened her eyes and saw Tommy Barnett. Tee. He sat across from her in a small room with a low ceiling and dirt floor, watching her. Had he felt the same way about Dell once? What had made him push Dell into doing what he did? Or was he just being protective toward Dell, the same way she'd been?

The difference was, Tommy would kill for Dell. And there was a good chance he knew that she'd been the one who'd fired the shots that had taken his best friend's life. *Her* best friend's. Was that why he'd kidnapped her daughter? Abducted *her?* Had he seen her shoot Dell that night?

She sat up, using the rough wall behind her for support, her eyes on Tommy Barnett.

"The game's almost over," he said. He leaned casually against the opposite wall, facing her. He didn't appear to be armed. He wore a baseball cap. Both of his hands were in the pockets of his jacket. "I was afraid you were going to miss the last inning."

Game? She heard the cheering then. The echo of the loudspeaker. Someone had just made a home run. She glanced around in confusion. They appeared to be in an old dugout.

She swallowed, her tongue feeling thick, dry as Texas dust. "Where is my daughter?" Her voice broke as all her fears welled up like tears inside her.

"She's at the ball game," he said matter-of-factly. "Where else would she be on a spring night like this?"

She frowned.

"Don't worry, you'll see her soon."

He seemed so...normal, she thought. Not like a kidnapper at all. Not even like a drug dealer. He looked like the boy next door.

"What is it you want?" she asked, sitting up a little straighter. Her head ached from where he'd hit her. "The money?"

"I make my own money," he said, waving off even the idea. "I'm just finishing what Dell started."

He made it sound as if he was talking about a project, like rebuilding an old car or refinishing a boat. Not about kidnapping a child. Not about murdering people.

"This is about his girlfriend, the one who was killed."

He nodded. "Amy. Dell loved her more than anything. They were going to get married right after graduation, couldn't wait. Then we were going to take over the barbecue joint so Bud and Lenore could have some fun. Dell'd always wanted that. His parents had worked so hard for so many years." He smiled. "Dell was going to make me a partner. We were going to franchise and open up H's Barbecue restaurants all over Texas. It would have worked, too." His smile faded.

"I don't understand."

"Frank Jordan killed Amy," Tommy said as if it all made perfect sense to him. She was sure it did. Because Frank had killed more than Dell's girlfriend. He'd killed the boys' dream, their planned futures.

She stared at Tommy, wondering desperately why she and Elena were a part of this. Frank was dying in a hospital in San Antonio. Maybe was already dead. Dell and Tommy had gotten their revenge. What more did Tommy want? Unless he'd seen her kill Dell. Was that what this was all about?

"What does my daughter have to do with this?" she asked, afraid of the answer.

He stared at her. "You really don't know?"

She felt her heart lurch.

"Dell always said how smart you were. He admired you a lot. He really liked you," Tommy assured her. "He said you were the best agent he'd ever met, because you were smart but you also cared. It tore him up knowing he had to kill you."

She thought of that moment of hesitation before Dell fired at her. It had cost him his life. But he *had* fired. He *would* have killed her. If she'd let him.

"Why?" she asked, tears welling in her eyes. "What was the point? All those years, working so hard to get into the FBI, getting put into Frank's division, why didn't Dell just kill him years ago?"

Tommy shook his head. "Dell always said that anything worth doing, was worth doing right. He wanted to get close to him, get to know him. He wanted Frank to know him as well. At first Dell was just going to gain his trust and then tell him who he was and execute him for murdering Amy, but then we realized how much help Dell could be to me in his position so we thought, why hurry?"

So Dell had been helping his drug-dealing friend. "Frank didn't mean to kill Amy. It was an accident in the line of duty," she said, but Tommy didn't seem to hear her.

"Then, Dell realized that killing Frank was almost like putting him out of his misery."

She stared at Tommy. It was true. The Frank Jordan she knew was not a happy man. She'd always thought it was Crystal's drinking that had made him that way. Now she wondered if Frank's unhappiness was what had caused Crystal's drinking. "His ex-wife told me that Frank never got over Amy's death.

Tommy shook his head. "It wasn't Amy who was eating him up inside. It was you."

"Me?"

"You still don't get it, do you? You figured out so much. Just like Dell said, you're smart. But you can't see what's been right in front of you the whole time. Just like Frank didn't see Dell."

She frowned as she looked up at Tommy, seized by a terrible premonition. Frank had covered up how Dell and Buster had died that night in the warehouse. It had never come out that they'd been shot by one of the other agents. Why had Frank done that?

Tommy nodded as if he could see her coming to the realization. "You were Frank's favorite. You wouldn't believe the strings he pulled to get you on his team. He was so proud of you. Dell said only a fool couldn't have seen it. Dell was no fool."

She swallowed, fear making her numb. Outside the dugout the crowd was screaming. Where was Elena? Somewhere out there watching the game? Eating popcorn, drinking a soda, waiting for her mommy and daddy to show up with Sweet Ana? Abby prayed so.

"What are you trying to tell me?" Her words came out in a hoarse whisper.

"Frank Jordan is your father."

Chapter Sixteen

Her father? Abby stared at Tommy. "My father died before I was born."

He shook his head. "Dell found out that Frank Jordan sent checks monthly to a woman named Ana Fuentes in Galveston, Texas."

The ground beneath her no longer felt solid. "No. That can't be. He'd have told me."

Tommy lifted a brow. "He ran out on your mother when she was pregnant with you. Why would he tell you that? Especially after your mother killed herself."

Her head spun. No. She wanted to argue. Dell had gotten it wrong. But she couldn't find the words. She remembered the way Jake had hesitated when she'd asked about her mother. She closed her eyes, unable to will it away. Frank. Her father. On some level, she knew it was true. The way her grandmother had never told her how her father and mother had died. Why they'd died so young.

And later, the way she'd gotten into the FBI and

quickly become part of Frank Jordan's team. The special treatment Frank had always given her. The odd argument they'd had the day of the explosion. The conversation they'd had in Study Butte. She *had* been his favorite and she'd known it. She just hadn't known why. Until now.

She let her gaze fall on Tommy's face. Oh, God. Now she understood. She understood it all. An eye for an eye. Take from Frank the one thing he valued most. Or in this case, the two things. His daughter and granddaughter.

She felt such a sudden sense of loss, not just for a father she hadn't known, but for the wasted years. Like Elena, she'd yearned for a father. There had been a time when she'd have given anything for one. Why had Frank walked out on her mother? Why had he never told her who he really was?

"I had hoped Frank would be here to see this," Tommy said. "But it will just have to be enough that he knew I'd taken his granddaughter before he died."

So much lost and for what? "Is Frank—"

"Dead?" Tommy shrugged. "One way or the other." He pulled a pistol from his jacket pocket and glanced out of the dugout. "The game is over. We'd better go get Elena." He motioned with the gun for her to lead the way.

She struggled to her feet, fighting back the grief, the loss, the fear. She had to think of Elena now. Elena had found *her* father and she'd be damned if she'd let anyone take that away from her. Jake would be on his way. She'd told him she was in Houston. And she knew Jake. He'd find her. Somehow. Even as she thought it, she knew it was inconceivable that he'd find her and Elena in a city this size. Even if he *could* get here in time.

But she wanted to see him, to look into his handsome face, to touch him again. After all these years they'd been apart, she couldn't bear the thought that she might not see him one more time.

"Don't plan on Jake," Tommy said as if he'd read her mind.

She looked back at him in surprise.

He smiled. "I figured you were thinking he'd be coming to your rescue soon." He shook his head. "Not this time."

JAKE FLEW into Houston in the dark, desperately trying to put all the pieces together quickly. Reese met him at the airport.

"You were right," Reese said as they hurried to the car. "The Texas Red Devils are playing at Bayview Field. It's about twenty minutes from here. You wanna drive?"

"No, you drive," Jake said getting into the passenger side. "You know Houston much better than I do."

Jake watched the city pass in a blur through his window. On the flight, he'd had a long time to think. Too long. Someone at the FBI had falsified the fingerprint and autopsy reports. Frank. But if he didn't have Elena, then why had he tried to make everyone think Abby was dead?

"Why would Frank lie about Abby's real identity?" he asked Reese.

Reese shrugged. "Maybe he got the wrong information. Or had some reason to not want anyone to know the truth."

Jake shook his head, remembering that moment of doubt when he'd heard the news. "You personally had the reports done, right?"

"Yeah, but Frank got wind of them," Reese said. "I didn't see the results until they'd gone through him."

Jake nodded. "What else did you find out about this Tommy Barnett?"

"Other than the fact that he's a drug dealer? Not much."

"Abby said he was a friend of Dell Harper's."

"Tommy Barnett *is* from Houston, Dell's old neighborhood."

"The same neighborhood we're headed for, right?"

Reese nodded. "You think he took Abby and Elena to the ball game?"

"Just a feeling," he said, praying his instincts were right. Dell had loved to play baseball. Jake recalled a photograph of Abby and Dell after a game, Dell's arm around Abby's shoulder, their heads close together, both smiling broadly. The memory clutched at his stomach.

Jake could kick himself now for not digging into

Dell's background, for not being more suspicious of the man. But he'd thought it was just jealousy that had made him suspect Dell, and hadn't listened to his instincts.

Reese turned into the baseball field parking lot and could see the ballpark ahead. It was deserted. His heart lunged in his chest. His instincts had been wrong. Or he hadn't gotten here in time.

"The game got out early," he said.

"No." Reese pointed to an adjacent ballpark where the lights still glowed on the field but only a couple of cars remained in the lot. "Looks like you're right on target."

As ABBY walked across the field, she saw that they were in an older field. The lights of another park shone down on the deep green of the diamond in the distance. Earlier she'd heard cars leaving, the sounds diminishing. Now the lights blinked off, pitching the park into darkness except for a shaft of light spilling out from beneath the concession area below the stands.

Under a moon cloaked in clouds, she walked ahead of Tommy across the dew-damp field, her eyes on the light, her heart pounding. Elena. *Oh God, let her be all right.* At that moment, she had just one wish. To hold her daughter in her arms. Even for one last time.

The stands stood empty and dark. Quiet settled over the ballpark and the humid spring night, as they crossed the deserted diamond.

Suddenly she spotted Elena in the dark bleachers. A man sat next to her. Elena waved excitedly when she saw her. The man rose and took Elena's hand. They started down the steps toward the field.

Her heart leapt into her throat at the sight of her daughter. All her FBI training hadn't prepared her for this. She knew better than to try to talk Tommy out of the finale he'd planned. His loyalty to Dell was unconditional. And she'd heard enough that night at the warehouse to know that it had been Tommy who had forced Dell to go through with his plot against Frank Jordan and Buster McNorton.

Nothing she could say would change Tommy's mind. She understood his commitment. While misplaced, it reminded her of the commitment she felt for her daughter. The same one she'd made years ago to Jake Cantrell. She would kill for Elena and Jake.

But she also knew that the odds of getting herself and Elena out of this weren't good. While she might be able to get the better of Tommy, she didn't stand much of a chance against two men.

And all the training in the world couldn't make her forget that this was her little girl running toward her. Her daughter who trusted and loved her without question.

She felt paralyzed at the thought of risking Elena's life. Because anything she did would be risky at best.

She glanced back at Tommy. He'd put the gun into his pocket again along with his hand. His look warned her to be very careful of what she did or said.

"Mommy!" Elena cried as she ran to her. "I flew in a helicopter all over and I got sick and threw up and I slept funny and I cried and I saw a baseball game and I ate hot dogs and popcorn and cotton candy and I so wanted my Sweet Ana and you, Mommy, and Daddy. They said you'd come. Where's Daddy? Why didn't he come with you?"

Abby fell to her knees and wrapped her arms around her baby, hugging her desperately. "Oh, Elena." What a resilient child, always finding that silver lining.

"I missed you, Mommy," Elena whispered.

"I missed you, too, *chica suena.*" She felt Tommy behind her.

"Let's go down to the concession stand," he said. She heard him take a deep breath. "Dell did love the game of baseball. He would have loved a night like this."

She heard the break in Tommy's voice, the anguish. As she pulled Elena up into her arms, she thought of Dell, the little brother she'd always wanted. "I loved Dell, too," she whispered and looked over at Tommy.

For an instant, their eyes met in the dim light. She saw his terrible pain, his remorse, his regret, his need for revenge at any price. It was a debt that had to be paid.

"Karl," he said to the man who'd been sitting with Elena. "Let's go check out the cotton candy."

She felt his hand on her arm. He pushed her toward the concession stand.

JAKE JUMPED out of the car and ran toward the ball-park, his heart thundering in his chest. He could hear Reese behind him, his limp slowing him down.

He drew his weapon as he neared the stands. From inside, he heard the tinkle of laughter. Elena's sweet laughter. And the sound of voices.

As he neared, he spotted something white lying on the ground. He bent down to pick up the baseball and stuffed it into his pocket without thinking. Slowly, he made his way toward the voices.

The air smelled of popcorn and fresh-mown grass. He slipped onto the field, moving along the edge of the stands. The voices grew more distinct as he neared the concession area. He stopped, glancing around for Reese, but he didn't see him. The ball field lay empty. Nothing moved on the breeze. No sounds other than the ones coming from beneath the stands.

He moved closer, weapon drawn.

"KARL, MAKE SURE we're not interrupted," Tommy said to the other man after he'd checked to make sure they were alone in the cool concrete concession area.

Karl nodded and moved to the bottom of the stairs leading up to the stands, his tread heavy and slow. The two men stood a few feet away, both facing her and Elena.

Abby hugged her daughter and looked around, hoping to see something she could use for a weapon, some way she could protect Elena. The room was large. Its cold concrete walls were painted with bright colors. A long line of metal counters ran the length of the room on the right. Nearer stood a cotton-candy machine. But not close enough that she could reach it.

Tommy stood for a moment, just looking around as if the room held a plethora of memories. Or he was waiting for something. But she knew he was watching her closely.

She lowered Elena to the floor, her hands on the child's small shoulders, half listening to her daughter recount the baseball game and the food she'd eaten. Half listening to Tommy's breathing.

His gaze finally settled on her and Elena.

Abby swallowed, praying for a miracle. It was the only thing that could save her and Elena now.

Tommy drew the pistol from his jacket. Elena's body stiffened beneath Abby's fingers.

Behind him and Karl, in the shadows, Abby thought she caught movement. She froze. Jake. He moved toward her, carefully sneaking up behind Tommy and Karl. If either of them turned, they would see him.

She met Jake's gaze, that old feeling arcing between them, strong as their passion for each other, strong as their need to save their daughter. Together. Just like old times.

"Stall," he mouthed.

"You realize that Dell was like a little brother to me," she said as she looked down the dark barrel of the pistol in Tommy's hand. "Dell—" The catch in her throat was real. "He was my best friend. I had no idea how much pain he was in. I just wish he'd told me. Maybe I could have helped."

Tommy shook his head. "There wasn't anything anyone could have done. Not from the moment Frank Jordan fired the shot that killed Amy."

Out of the corner of her eye, she saw Jake pull a baseball from his pocket. He motioned to her.

"Anything you want me to tell Dell when I see him?" she asked quickly.

Tommy seemed taken back by her question.

The instant Jake threw the ball, she cried, "Under the counter!" in Spanish to Elena and hurled the child toward the metal concessions. Abby dove after her.

The ball hit Tommy in the back. He let out a loud "Ufft!" and got off a wild shot as he stumbled and fell to his knees from the blow.

Abby rolled as gunfire ricocheted through the concession area. She came up behind the cotton-candy machine. Karl had turned and fired at Jake. She drove the cotton-candy machine into the thug's side as she scrambled to her feet, driving Karl back. Jake fired. Karl dropped like a rock, his pistol rattling to the floor.

She grabbed his gun and swung around.

Tommy was gone.

Behind her, she caught a glimpse of Elena scrambling toward a large cooler. Tommy came around the end of the counter and grabbed Elena before Abby could get off a shot.

"Jake!" she cried as Tommy came up too quickly with Elena in his arms, the barrel of his pistol to the back of the child's head.

"Drop the gun," he ordered. "Now!"

She let the pistol fall to the floor.

"You too, Jake," Tommy said as he moved from behind the counter, using Elena as a shield. The child's eyes were wide but lit up when she spied her father.

"Daddy!" she cried.

"Hi, baby," he said. "Everything's going to be fine." He lowered his gun to the floor and stepped away from it as Tommy instructed. The room grew impossibly quiet.

"Dell wouldn't have wanted this," she said, knowing she was wasting her breath.

With a shudder of relief she saw Reese appear behind Tommy. He limped toward them, his weapon drawn.

"Reese?" Tommy said at the limping sound behind him. "What kept you? I could have used some help."

"Looks like you're doing just fine," Reese said.

She heard Jake swear under his breath behind her as Elena squirmed in Tommy's hold.

She stared at Reese. Hadn't he been the one who'd given Jake the cell phone with the tracking device in it? The one who'd told Jake she wasn't

Abby Diaz? He'd made them believe Frank was behind it. Frank, her father. Could what Crystal have told her be true?

"I should have known," Jake said. "If I hadn't figured out that Abby was here, you would have helped me out, huh, Reese? You've been so helpful. Like the cell phone with the tracking device. Nice touch."

Reese shrugged and gave a slight bow. "I do try to please."

"And telling me that Abby really wasn't Abby," Jake said as he moved up behind her and put a hand on her back. "That was good!" She realized it wasn't just his hand. He pressed the cold steel of a knife flat to her back. She reached back, as if to cover his hand with her own, and took the knife and slipped it down into the waistband of her jeans. "You have a flare for the dramatic!"

"Please, you're making me blush," Reese said. "Now, kindly step away from Abby." He motioned with his gun.

Jake stepped a few feet away from her in Tommy's direction. A clear signal. She'd recognized the knife as well. It was the one she'd pulled from Julio's body, the one she'd had in her bag. She knew, the same way she knew Reese didn't know Jake had had the knife.

"But you did figure it out," the agent said. "You just thought Frank was behind it. Him putting the tracking device in the cell phone made it so easy for me."

"Don't tell me you're doing this for Dell Harper, too," Jake said conversationally.

Reese shook his head. "Naw, I'm just in it for the money. Crass, huh?" He shrugged. "The thing about being on a drug task force, you see so much money and after a while you realize if you put one drug dealer away, another one just comes along to take his place. What's the point?"

"That's bull, Reese, and you know it," Jake said congenially enough. "It's greed, plain and simple."

Reese's look darkened. "The FBI owes me something for this bum leg."

"The FBI didn't blow up that warehouse," Abby interjected.

"Enough already," Tommy snapped. "Let's get this over with."

She had to get Elena away from Tommy. "Please, just let me hold my baby one last time. Then you can—do what it is you have to do."

"Don't do it," Reese warned. "You don't know her like I do. She might try something."

Tommy shot Reese a disgusted look. "Like what? She isn't armed and she can't do much with a child in her arms."

He slowly let Elena down, turning the pistol on Jake. "And I'll be forced to kill her lover and the father of her baby if she does." Elena ran to her.

She scooped her daughter into her arms and hugged her tightly, aware of the knife wedged against her spine.

"Keep your hands where I can see them," Reese warned Jake.

She waited for a sign from Jake.

"You're getting awfully paranoid, Ramsey," he said.

Now! With one swift desperate move, she held Elena with one arm and reached back with her free hand, pulled the knife and threw it in a once expert, long-practiced movement. It appeared knife throwing was right up there with bike riding. You never quite forgot how.

The blade glittered in the concession lights for an instant, then hit home, burying itself to the hilt in Reese's chest.

Reese gasped in surprise and stumbled back, getting off a wild shot that ricocheted through the room.

Abby whirled around, trying to shield Elena, as she dove for the stairs.

At that same instant, Jake went for Tommy's weapon.

A shot echoed through the building. Then another. She waited for the pain as she clutched her daughter to her breast and launched herself and Elena under the stairs.

For a moment, she thought she might have been hit. She stared down at Elena, seeing the wide eyes, but feeling the child's sweet breath against her cheek as she pulled her back under the open stairwell.

Silence filled the concession area. She waited with her heart lodged in her throat. She had no weapon. And she and Elena were trapped.

"It's all right, Abby."

She felt tears rush her eyes at the sound of Jake's voice. It was over.

Slowly she climbed out with Elena. Tommy lay on the floor at an odd angle. Blood leaked out like motor oil onto the concrete. Reese was sprawled not far away, his weapon still in his hand, his eyes open and sightless, the same knife that had killed Julio stuck in his chest. There was something symbolic about that, she thought.

She turned away, shielding Elena, and felt Jake's arm come around her shoulders.

"Daddy!" Elena cried as she encircled his neck with her arms. "I knew you'd come. I wasn't even scared."

Jake hugged them both to him, then led them up the stairs and out into the night.

"The thing is," Jake said as they walked across the ballfield. "I have this place north of here on the Smoking Barrel Ranch where I work. Right now the cabin isn't much but I was thinking, we could always add on to it."

Abby looked up. The first star of the night glittered brightly in a sky warm and rich with the promise of summer. She stumbled to a stop, realization rushing over her in a drowning wave of relief. Tears blurred the night and great sobs rose in her chest. They were alive. They were together. At last.

Jake pulled her and Elena into his arms. The three of them stood in the middle of the baseball diamond, cloaked in the darkness as the rest of the stars came out, one after another.

Chapter Seventeen

Frank Jordan had come out of his coma. He was asking for his daughter.

"This is something I need to do alone," Abby told Jake. She reached up to cup his jaw in her hand. His face was warm, his dark eyes full of promise.

She stood on tiptoe to meet his kiss. It fired that now-familiar passion. Just a look. A touch. A whisper. She wondered if she would always yearn for him and suspected she would until the day she died.

"I'll take Elena to the park across street," he offered. "Take your time. You can meet us there."

She smiled and squeezed his hand, then knelt down to hug her daughter. She still feared letting Elena and Jake out of her sight, but she knew she had to learn to trust again. To believe that they'd lived through this for a reason. And that now, nothing could keep them apart.

As she stepped gingerly into Frank's room, she was filled with so many emotions. And even more regrets.

He looked older against the white of the pillow, his face drawn and pale. But his eyes lit up when he saw her and tears welled and spilled down his cheeks.

She moved to his bedside.

"I'm so sorry," he whispered. "If I had married your mother—" His voice broke.

She sat down in the chair next to his bed. He reached for her hand. It felt cold, as cold as her heart toward him. "Tell me about you and my mother."

Slowly, he proceeded to tell her a story of a young, ambitious man and a beautiful Mexican girl named Rosa Louisa. Her mother. He faltered when he reached the part where Rosa Louisa told him she was pregnant with his child.

"I made the biggest mistake of my life," he said, his voice no more than a whisper. "I abandoned her. I thought a wife and a child would keep me from reaching my dreams." Anguish contorted his face. "I have regretted leaving your mother every day of my life."

"You could have gone back," she said, wishing that were true.

He shook his head. "She wasn't strong. She took her life right after you were born. I never got to tell her how I felt. How sorry I was."

"Why didn't you come for me?" Abby asked, her heart breaking.

He shook his head. "You were better off with your grandmother."

"But still, you could have—"

"I couldn't face you with the truth. Not then, not later." He told her how he'd watched her from a distance, watched her grow up. How he'd planted the seed about the FBI when he'd sent her career information after graduation. How delighted he'd been when she'd unknowingly followed in her father's footsteps, becoming an FBI agent. No wonder her grandmother had been so upset about that choice.

"I couldn't believe it when I had the chance to get you on my team," he said. "I was so proud of you. To be near you—"

"That day I disappeared, you called me in your office."

He nodded. "I was worried about you. I'd seen how protective you were with Dell."

"Did you know about Dell?"

He shook his head. "I knew you were pregnant with my grandchild." He waved away her question of how he'd known. "I just didn't want anything to happen to the two of you."

"You covered up what happened." It sounded like an accusation even to her ears.

"I did what I thought was best. It wasn't until later that I put it all together and realized it was my fault. That Dell had ultimately killed you and the baby because of me. But I thought it was over."

All he'd had after that was his work, he said. He'd thrown himself into it. Crystal began to drink more, feeling disconnected from him, and they'd finally divorced. His fault. She'd realized all his emotions were tied up in the past and the family he'd lost.

"Then you really didn't know Julio Montenegro abducted me?" Abby asked.

"No, I was knocked out in the blast. I believed the body we found in the ashes was yours. I never dreamed you might be alive. Until Julio contacted me. He'd been there that night. He'd taken you and the knowledge of what had happened to use when he had enough money to make a move against Calderone."

"I only found three hundred thousand dollars," she said.

"Who knows how much he stole?" Frank said. "I have a feeling Ramon knew a lot more about Calderone's missing money than Julio. I would imagine Ramon used Julio as his scapegoat."

"Ramon?"

"Dead. Killed in the shootout in Study Butte."

"You saved my life and Elena's," she said, knowing that now to be true.

"I'm the one who jeopardized it in the first place," he said bitterly. "I did everything I could to protect you, including hiring Jake to go after you. He was the one man I believed I could trust although I'd been given evidence to the contrary. I knew Jake. I knew how much he loved you. If he couldn't get you and Elena out of Mexico alive, no one could."

"You also falsified the fingerprint and autopsy reports," she said.

He nodded. "I thought if no one knew you were Abby Diaz—"

"But Tommy knew."

He nodded. "Because of Reese."

He'd even made a deal with the devil, Calderone, providing the information where Ramon could find Jake in Study Butte. In exchange, he got to call the shots.

But things had gone badly at Study Butte because he hadn't known about Tommy Barnett. Nor about Reese.

"How did you know about Study Butte?" she asked, remembering that Jake thought no one had.

Frank looked chagrined. "When you started seeing him, I found out *everything* about him. I'm also the one who put the tracking device in the cell phone Reese gave Jake. I thought I could protect you."

He'd acted like a caring father, she thought. She squeezed his hand, touched by his attempts to protect her and Elena. He'd risked his life. He'd even risked his job, his reputation with the Bureau, something that had meant so much to him.

"We're fine," she said. "Elena is—" She shook her head and smiled, not sure how to describe her daughter. "She bounces back easily. It's as if she came into the world expecting nothing, so she's always amazed by what life has to offer her." Tears filled her eyes. "She has the father she's always wanted. She'll mend."

Frank squeezed her hand. "I would like to be part of your lives, but I know I have no right to ask."

Abby looked into his face, her feelings all too close to the surface. "We're going to need some time. Jake is taking us up to the Smoking Barrel Ranch where he works. He has a place up there on Ash Pond. Elena loves it. He's promised to teach her to ride. And the people on the ranch, well, they're quite the bunch. They've become Jake's family."

He nodded. "I understand."

She got to her feet. "The thing is," she said, feeling tears rush her eyes. "Elena would love having a grandfather."

"What about you, Abby? Is it too late for us to be father and daughter?"

Was it ever too late to find the father you'd always yearned for? "I was thinking," she said, hearing her voice break, "you might like the Smoking Barrel Ranch and I know you'd find the people who live there very interesting. Maybe when you're feeling better, you could come up."

He burst into a smile, his eyes swimming in tears. "I'll do that."

Epilogue

From the porch of the Smoking Barrel Ranch, Jake watched the helicopter touch down on the front lawn. Behind him in the house, he could hear Rosa and Elena in a discussion about what to make for dessert. Jake only half listened to their running conversation. They were both speaking in lightning-speed Spanish, as Elena trailed along behind the good-natured cook.

He watched as a man jumped down from the chopper and, keeping low, ran toward the house.

Behind him, the rugged Texas plains ran to the vast horizon. The waning sun turned the distant Davis Mountains to pale purple.

The federal agent stopped at the bottom of the porch steps. ''The new director asked that I see you get this personally.'' He held out a large manila envelope marked Confidential.

Jake took it and, with a slight nod, the man retreated to the helicopter. Once he was back inside, it lifted off again. Jake watched until the chopper was no more than a dark speck against the pale sky.

He turned at the sound of footsteps behind him as Abby came through the screen door to join him. She was dressed in jeans, boots and a western shirt that hugged her lush curves. He pulled her to him, thinking about the baby growing inside her. Their child. A sister for Elena. Or a brother. Not that it mattered. They'd have more children. Maybe they'd fill this old ranch house.

They'd already outgrown his cabin on the acreage he'd bought from Mitchell. The place sat overlooking Ash Pond and now rang with the sounds of laughter and little girl giggles. He'd been working all summer on an addition, excited about the nursery he'd built and Abby had decorated.

"What is it?" she asked when she noticed the envelope in his hand.

"The original reports on the fingerprints from the handcuffs, the autopsy on the body in Abby Diaz's grave and DNA on Elena," he said.

"You haven't opened it?"

He leaned down and kissed her. "I already know everything I need to know. How about you?"

She looked up at him and shook her head as she wrapped her arms around his neck.

"I love you, Abby," he whispered against her hair. "After dinner I intend to show you just how much."

She laughed and curled into the crook of his arm as they headed back into the house. Her memory had returned. And along with it, her love for him. It blazed in her eyes, in her touch. He couldn't quit looking at her. He especially couldn't quit touching her. It had taken a while, but he was finally beginning to believe that Abby and Elena were safe.

As he opened the screen door and drew her inside the house, he tossed the envelope on the table. Elena came running, wrapping herself around their legs.

"We're going to have flan for dessert. Rosa said I could help. I get to break the eggs and stir and I helped with the enchiladas. Rosa says I'm a great cook."

Jake laughed as he ran a hand over the child's sleek black hair. She'd blossomed since they'd arrived at the ranch. He'd never seen a child like her. She amazed him every day and thrilled him. He had never known such love. Except for the love he felt for her mother.

He glanced up to see that most everyone had gathered in the kitchen. He could smell enchiladas cooking in the oven, Elena's favorite, and hear their neighbor Maddie Wells arguing with Mitchell about his health.

"He doesn't take care of himself," Maddie called after Mitchell as he came out into the foyer. He winked at Jake and Abby as he passed.

"The woman loves me," Mitchell said, shaking his head.

His impossible executive assistant Penny Archer trailed right behind him, complaining that someone had been in her computer files. "We need better security around here, Mitchell."

Jake led the way into the big, bright country kitchen, his arm still around Abby, Elena riding along on the tops of his boots. Catharine, Brady Morgan's new bride, was making a salad, or at least trying to. Brady couldn't seem to leave her alone. Rosa was laughing at something Slim, their Romeo of a ranch hand, had said, her face flushed.

Jake pulled out a chair for Abby, then drew one up for himself as he pulled Elena onto his lap. His heart swelled at the sight of his family.

IN THE OTHER ROOM, Penny picked up the manila envelope marked Confidential from the front table. "Isn't this the proof the FBI promised on Abby and Elena?"

Mitchell nodded.

"Jake didn't even open it," she said.

Mitchell smiled as he looked back into the kitchen. "Jake knows everything he needs to know." He took the envelope from her and tossed it into the fireplace. The flames quickly devoured the pages.

Penny gasped as she watched them burn.

"Mitchell, you might want to hear this," Maddie called from the kitchen. "Jake has an announcement."

Mitchell offered his arm to his assistant.

Penny took it but mugged a face at him as she did. "What now?" she grumbled.

"Oh, I have a pretty good idea," he said. "I'd suggest you get busy and learn how to knit baby booties."

"Not likely," she groaned. "I have enough to do around here."

"Abby and I are getting married," Jake announced when they were all in the large ranch kitchen. He turned to Abby and, reaching into his pocket, pulled out a heart-shaped locket on a silver chain. The silver gleamed as he put the locket around her neck. "She's said she'll have me."

Everyone applauded but he held up a hand to silence them. "That's not all," he said with a laugh. "Elena is going to have a brother or sister come next spring." He smiled at Abby and Elena. Mitchell had never seen him so happy.

Elena cheered and clapped. "Mommy says I can be a flower girl and dance with Daddy at the wedding and wear a really pretty dress." She danced around the room, then stopped as a thought hit her. "I want a brother *and* a sister *and* a horse."

Everyone laughed.

"Anyone seen Rafe?" Cody, the youngest agent, asked from the doorway. Rafael "Rafe" Alvarez was the charmer of all the agents, Cody often the sullen, moody one.

"He's out riding patrol, why?" Slim asked.

Cody shook his head. "What's going on here?"

"Just the usual," Mitchell said as he let his gaze fall on his ever-growing family. "This calls for a toast."

He broke out the champagne and filled glasses, promising Maddie he'd only have a little.

He lifted his glass. It surprised him, the lump he felt in his throat as he looked around the room. He wished Rafe was here for this. And Daniel Austin, the agent they'd lost last year.

He touched his glass to Maddie's. "To everlasting love."

*   *   *   *   *

You've read the first two books of
TEXAS CONFIDENTIAL.
Now don't miss book three,

THE SPECIALIST
by Dani Sinclair

Available next month wherever
Harlequin Intrigues are sold.

For a special preview of
THE SPECIALIST,

turn the page...
And let the excitement
and passion begin!

Prologue

Silence stilled even the chirp of crickets. Whicker suddenly lifted his head and stared into the darkness. The creak of leather cracked the silence as Rafe Alvarez sat up straighter in the saddle, coming fully alert. He stroked Whicker's sleek neck and whispered softly, instantly quieting the massive gelding.

For months the rustlers had seemed to know exactly when and where to strike. They either had the luck of the devil, or they had inside information on the placement of the ranch hands.

Rafe set his jaw. The possibility festered in all their minds. After what his fellow Texas Confidential agent Jake and his wife Abby had gone through because of a mole inside the FBI, tension was heightened for all of the agents at the Smoking Barrel Ranch, the headquarters of Texas Confidential. Protecting the cattle around the clock on a ranch this size was impossible, especially since the Smoking Barrel was being deliberately and systematically targeted. No doubt Calderone, an infamous drug lord they had been trying to nab for months, was behind the problem, but that begged the question—who else did the drug lord have on his payroll?

Backing his horse into a stand of scrub pines Rafe waited, his hand hovering over the rifle stock. He welcomed this instant rush of adrenaline after the tedious hours of waiting and watching. Rafe liked being a working cowboy, as well as a Texas Confidential agent. So did his colleagues. And none of them liked the strain they'd been working under lately. Rafe welcomed action at this point—any action that would result in the capture of the men responsible for the rustling that had plagued the ranch recently, and bring them one step closer to Calderone.

Any moment now, the rustlers would break out over the ridge and be silhouetted clearly against the cooperative moon before the encroaching clouds could darken the landscape once more.

The sound of a hoof striking rock gave him final confirmation. Whicker took several mincing sidesteps, sensing Rafe's tension. He too was eager for action. Rafe soothed him silently as they waited.

A horse and rider abruptly broke the ridge in an easy, almost sanguine canter. Rafe frowned. Rider singular. And this would-be rustler was entirely too confident. Rafe watched him come to a stop at the top of the ridge, pausing to survey the cattle below as if he had every right to be there. The man sat tall, his hat pulled low. With the moon at the stranger's back, Rafe couldn't make out any features, but he did catch a reflection beneath the brim. The man wore glasses.

The wind abruptly shifted. The rustler's paint picked up Whicker's scent. The smaller horse whinnied a greeting, alerting his rider. The man swiveled to peer at the lone stand of pines.

Rafe dropped his hand from the rifle butt and gently kicked Whicker into a gallop. The well-trained cutting horse gathered himself without effort and sprang forward, even as the rustler whirled, urging his horse into a reckless plunge back down the incline.

Was the fool trying to kill himself?

The rustler had the advantage of the lead, but Whicker's training and much longer stride made the outcome a given. The smaller paint didn't stand a chance of outrunning him, though his rider tried. The distance between the two horses closed quickly. It was obvious that the other rider wasn't going to stop as the two horses thundered dangerously down the embankment, right toward the grazing cattle herd.

A cloud drifted across the moon, darkening the night as Rafe pulled alongside the other rider. The rustler twisted around for a look just as Rafe came abreast. Rafe kicked free of the stirrups and lunged. Like a choreographed movie stunt, momentum carried both of them to the hard packed earth in a bone-jarring fall. Hats went flying as they rolled several feet before coming to a stop.

Rafe found himself lying full length along the

other's skinny form. His hand had come to rest inside the intruder's open jacket front. He was stunned to recognize the softly rounded curve beneath his hand for what it was.

"A girl?"

She gave him a shove. "A woman," she corrected with haughty disdain.

Her voice flowed over him like warm brandy as she tried to adjust the glasses that were hanging half off her face.

"Rafael Alvarez, I presume?"

Stunned, Rafe could only nod.

Her mouth tightened in a line of anger right before her fist landed against his jaw with enough force to hurt more than his pride. She scrambled out from beneath him, rising to her feet.

"Next time, watch where you put your hands." She regarded him with narrowed eyes and began dusting off her jeans.

"Who *are* you?" he demanded.

"I'm Kendra Kincaide—your new partner."

Chapter One

Rafe rose slowly, rubbing his jaw. He was going to have a bruise! In fact, she might just have loosened a couple of his teeth—but he'd be hanged before he'd admit that out loud.

"My partner, huh?" He surveyed her lanky, boyish build beneath the dark jacket she wore and the no-nonsense glasses that still hung askew on her narrow face after their tumble. Rafe suddenly found himself wanting to grin. Whoever she was, she was no rustler.

"Darlin', most women who want to be my 'partner' use a slightly different approach."

Her lips thinned in prissy rejection of his attempt to tease. "Not *that* sort of partner."

"Well, I'm not into rustlin' cattle, darlin'," he offered.

"I'm not a cattle thief!"

"Well certainly not the sort I was expectin'," he agreed watching her closely. It was difficult to tell in the dark, but he'd swear she was blushing. Now when had he ever seen a grown woman blush? Was she so naive she didn't realize the risk of running around the countryside in the middle of the night by herself?

"What are you doing out here at this hour, darlin'?" he asked, taking a step in her direction. Instantly, she backed away, almost stumbling over a rock.

"Stop that!"

Rafe halted. He was used to a much different reaction from the women he met and he found himself unaccountably irritated by her angry response and this entire crazy situation. Somebody needed to teach Ms. Kendra Kincaide that there could be consequences to foolish actions.

"No call to be shy, darlin'. There's only you and me and the cattle out here." He swept his hand to indicate their isolation and caught a glimpse of Whiskers munching contentedly on some grass a few yards away.

"Shy? Why you arrogant—" She fumbled for words, obviously at a loss. "Male," she finally spit at him.

Rafe rubbed his jaw where her fist had connected. "Guilty."

Her eyes glinted in the moonlight reflected off the unattractive glasses she wore. Any minute now, like a cartoon, steam would pour from beneath the open collar of her jacket. She was too annoyed to be frightened, but she should be frightened. Didn't she see the risk out here in the pre-dawn morning hours?

Rafe closed the distance between them. This time, she held her ground. Overhead, clouds parted to let the moon highlight her features.

Thirtyish, at a guess, though her age was hard to determine for sure. Her brown hair was long and stringy. The ends looked as if she'd taken dull scissors to them. No jewelry, not even a ring. He continued his assessment, waiting for her reaction. Dark jeans hugged a surprisingly nice pair of legs, and a light colored, button-down shirt that he'd already discovered harbored a nicely rounded pair of breasts. Her feet had been stuffed into a pair of boots that looked suspiciously new. She had surprisingly small feet.

"If you're through with the inventory, you can hold it right there, buster."

She might not be much to look at, but she did have spunk, he decided.

"Buster?"

She set her jaw, planted her fists on her hips and glared at him. "Your name is Rafael Alvarez," she snapped out. "But you're called Rafe. Six feet one inch tall, brown hair, green eyes, half Spanish and half Irish," she recited. "And all baloney," she added defiantly.

"Baloney?"

"Your parents died in a car crash when you were an infant. Your grandparents raised you until your freshman year of college. Tragically, they died along with a lot of other people in that fire on board the cruise ship Althea."

His amusement dissolved at her recital.

"Their deaths left you alone, but financially secure," she continued. "You went back to school where you got in with a rowdy crowd. Your sophomore year culminated in your drunken arrest for grand theft auto. A friend boosted another friend's car before picking you and several young females up after a party. All of you were drunk and there was beer in the car."

Rafe flinched at the memory.

"Fortunately, the police stopped the driver before anyone was hurt. You spent a full night in jail and hired a high-priced lawyer to avoid serious criminal charges. Apparently, you wised up after that. You dropped your former associates, changed your major and went on to study law, though you never took the bar exam."

How did she know all this? Rafe thought angrily.

"That's enough." His soft voice tone would have warned off anyone who knew him. Kendra never batted an eye.

"Next, you applied to the police academy, but you were too much of a maverick for all their rules and regulations. You dropped out almost right away. Or maybe they suggested you leave. Either way, you did some research of your own. I'm guessing you stumbled over the very quiet, very private organization known as Texas Confidential."

Rafe drew in a breath, his body vibrating with sudden tension. "I'll ask you again. Who *are* you?"

"We already covered that. Then—"

He grabbed her shoulders in a punishing grip. Instantly, he relaxed his hold because she felt astonishingly delicate beneath his broad hands. While he wanted to scare her enough to interrupt her recital, he didn't want to hurt her. Her eyes widened behind her glasses giving her a frightened, baby owl appearance.

Rafe gentled his hold even further when she licked her lips nervously. He followed the motion of her tongue, annoyed to notice that she had very nice lips—when they weren't pursed in disdain.

"I want to know who you are."

"I told you," she stated boldly, "I'm Kendra Kincaide."

He crowded her until she was pressed along his jacket. The action defined her slenderness against his much larger masculinity. He watched her eyes widen in final acknowledgement of his size and gender and their isolation. Nearby, a cow snorted at a patch of ground.

"Who is Kendra Kincaide?" he asked softly.

She lifted her chin a little higher, though she flinched when he took the back of his hand and ran it down the side of her face. He felt her body quiver. The softness of her skin took him by surprise yet again. Her long, unstylish hair tumbled messily about her shoulders while a beguiling scent of shampoo filled his nostrils. She wasn't his type by a long shot. Still, he found himself aware that she was definitely a woman. That firm round curve of flesh he'd held so fleetingly had left an indelible impression.

Some of her assertiveness drained away as he continued to hold her shoulders now. She licked her lips once more and planted her hands on her hips. "I told you I'm—"

"My partner," he finished for her. Time for her to comprehend the risk she was taking. He trailed his fingers over the curve of her cheek, sliding them along the slope of her neck to where the vee of her open jacket revealed the cotton material of her blouse. "But if you know so much about me, you know I prefer selecting my own—*partners.*"

Rafe didn't feel the least bit sorry for using his own brand of intimidation. The woman was playing a dangerous game of some sort. A game that could have serious consequences if she tried this approach on the wrong man. He let his fingers slide beneath the top button of her blouse in a subtle warning caress.

For a moment, neither of them moved. The abrupt prick of the knife tip against his exposed throat came as a complete shock.

"Back up, Alvarez. I mean it." There was nothing teasing in her tone.

While it would have been a simple matter to take the knife from her, Rafe was more curious than alarmed. This was not the effect his legendary charm generally had on women. Of course, he wasn't exerting a whole lot of charm right now. Still, no other woman had ever caught him so totally off guard as this skinny handful of a female with the glittering eyes.

Rafe dropped his hand and took a step back, watching her intently.

"Do I make you that nervous, darlin'?"

"No, you annoy me that much."

The knife disappeared with a speed that made him pay attention. She was not what she seemed.

"And stop calling me darling!"

His lips curved at the corners. "Whatever you say, sugar."

Kendra Kincaide looked like she wanted to stomp her booted feet—preferably in the region of his face. Rafe found his lips curving in a reluctant smile that disappeared almost as fast as it had come. He rocked back on his heels, hooked his thumbs in his belt and studied her.

"I assume you're going to explain why and how you know so much about me?"

Kendra shook the hair out of her face and kept from sighing her relief out loud. Thankfully, he'd finally given her some breathing space. She wasn't used to being crowded—and he was a very large man.

"Your life is an open book," she told him.

"Is that right?"

SHE TOLD HERSELF she was edgy because she didn't appreciate the way he studied her like some tasty morsel waiting to be sampled. The truth was, she'd been totally unprepared to meet Rafael Alvarez in the flesh.

He looked deceptively relaxed as he nudged his

hat farther back on his forehead with a knuckle and regarded her. He was toying with her, darn him. The knowledge annoyed her.

"It is for anyone who knows how to operate a computer keyboard," she affirmed.

"And you do."

"It's what I do best."

"Now that," he said suggestively, sweeping her body once more with his gaze, "is too bad. There are lots of better things a woman like you should do best."

The moonlight allowed her to see his gently mocking expression. She'd studied his computer image for hours. She'd thought she knew every nuance of his features, but nothing could have prepared her for the sensual reality of the man himself.

Rafe Alvarez was bigger, more masculine, and far sexier than any picture could convey. His suave, rumbly voice slipped inside her mind like a phantom lover's caress.

She wasn't supposed to be feeling this pull of attraction, yet her skin still felt the path his hand, then his fingers, had taken down her face and below. Her heart still hadn't settled back to a regular rhythm. This would never do. The key to handling a man like Rafe was to keep the upper hand. He was baiting her, but two could play at that game.

"I know everything about you and Mitchell Forbes and his Texas Confidential agents," she asserted. "I even know your next assignment." She watched his body tighten. "You're going after Stephen Rialto."

She dangled the name between them in the silence of the night, disturbed only by the distant shuffle of the herd of cattle.

Rafe's eyes narrowed dangerously. A shiver traced its way down her spine at his new expression. Despite the sensuality that practically radiated from him, this was not a man to trifle with.

"What do you know about Stephen Rialto?" Rafe asked softly.

"More than I want to know." She knew he saw the small shudder she couldn't control. "He's lower than a snake and far more deadly. I intend to help you see that justice is served."

THE SECRET IS OUT!

HARLEQUIN®

I N T R I G U E®

presents

By day these agents are cowboys;
by night they are specialized
government operatives.
Men bound by love, loyalty and the law—
they've vowed to keep their missions
and identities confidential....

Harlequin Intrigue

Harlequin American Romance
(a special tie-in story)

HARLEQUIN®

Makes any time special ™